THE
MARBLE
CURSE

RICHARD VINCENT

The Book Guild Ltd

First published in Great Britain in 2021 by
The Book Guild Ltd
9 Priory Business Park
Wistow Road, Kibworth
Leicestershire, LE8 0RX
Freephone: 0800 999 2982
www.bookguild.co.uk
Email: info@bookguild.co.uk
Twitter: @bookguild

This work is entirely fictitious and bears no resemblance to any persons living or dead.

Typeset in 12pt Adobe Jenson Pro

Printed and bound in the UK by TJ Books Ltd, Padstow, Cornwall

ISBN 978 1913551 674

British Library Cataloguing in Publication Data.
A catalogue record for this book is available from the British Library.

CONTENTS

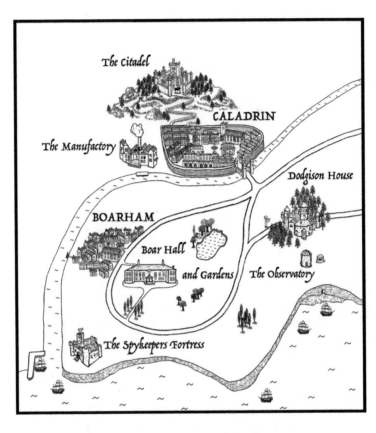

MAP OF CALADRIN AND BOARHAM

CHAPTER 1

UNEXPECTED PRESENTS

Staring out of his window, Joe Raven was controlling his latest invention. As it flew over his garden, he checked its solar-electric shell, eye cameras and jet-propelled legs. He had been an inventor since he was three, starting with a secret trapdoor in his kitchen table to make his peas disappear without eating them. Now, aged eleven, wiry and with dark copper hair, he was famous as a master of small gadgets that had extraordinary power.

To bring his ideas to life he had made his bedroom into a 'Creatory'. It was impossibly full. Screens and machines, clips and chips, glues and screws, cool tools and hot irons all had their place – not to mention the 277 well-labelled boxes of essential supplies. The walls were covered with shelved bottles and jars, mostly labelled 'Poison'. He still slept there, though the only space left for sleep was between the rafters under his floor that he reached through a sliding panel with voice control.

At the same time, his sister, Beth, was giving a speech to her bedroom mirror. She was two years older than Joe and more solid. Her chocolate-brown hair, when not pinned up, fell in shallow curls to her shoulders. Books covered her floor as well as filling her shelves. They also struggled for space on top of her wardrobe. One shelf was set aside for her trophies. The shield of a Junior Master Bowman of FAST – the Field Archery Society of Trembleton – was displayed in the centre. In drama, her other great pastime, she was three-time winner of the SPIT Cup for her Solo Performance in Theatre. Now she was practising for her next leading role.

Beth usually kept well away from Joe's Creatory, but her mirror reflected the impossible sight of a mysterious flying animal. Curiosity drove her to brave a visit. Slowly, she opened his door. The air was sharp. It made her breathing hurt, and it was changing colour. A flame was burning dangerously on a windowsill.

'Joe, there's purple smoke in here and the curtain is going to catch fire!' she shouted.

'It's the iodine. Turn the gas out, please. I'm making a landing.'

She covered her mouth and nose, blinked hard, and killed the flame. 'I've just seen an odd flying creature outside,' she said after her throat had recovered.

No response.

'Another marvel of Trembleton's nimble-fingered inventor?'

'… er… Yes.' Joe's brain stayed bolted to a screen while he commanded his flight-control app to prepare for landing. 'Touch-down. That's it! A brilliant maiden flight of the first-ever Spy-tortoise!'

'A flying tortoise that's a spy? Do you think someone might notice it in the air?'

'It sneaks around on the ground most of the time. Flying is for a quick getaway.'

'Of course… Did it spy anything?'

'An old cardboard box under the tree.'

'An old cardboard box? Surely not! A threat to humankind, right on our doorstep?'

'Well, it wasn't there ten minutes ago—'

'Perhaps it was dropped by Father on the way to his office.'

A revolting smell of decay suddenly made Beth sneeze. 'What putrefaction is this?' She pointed to a round glass dish lying by Joe's jars.

'Bioluminescent bacteria. They glow in the dark. I thought you might like them as a nightlight.'

'Oh no, young Sir, though 'tis a kindly offering. But sickly germs next to my pillow? A truly frightening prospect for a young lady with a sensitive disposition – and for a mother for whom even the *word* "germ" ignites horror and a desperate search for disinfectant.'

'Your loss,' said Joe, used to Beth's outbursts of drama.

'But I remain deeply grateful.'

'Shall I—'

A screeching 'Meow!' came from downstairs – the CREAM, Joe's Cat Re-Entry Alarm Monitor.

'That's Copurrnicus. I'll go,' he said.

As soon as the back door opened, a fluffy ginger cat flashed past him into the kitchen. Usually he would have chased it, but he stopped to look at the package his Spy-tortoise had spotted under the tree. About three times bigger than a shoe box, it was tied up with rough string held by red sealing wax. He picked it up. It was as light as a balloon. He shook it. Nothing rattled, squeaked or sploshed. Odd. How had it got there? His father definitely wouldn't have dropped it and the garden had no outside gate. He studied the grass: no footprints, no marks. No one was hiding in the tree. He looked at it again and discovered a small, handwritten label. What he saw made him run to the kitchen where Beth was reading and his mother, as usual, was talking to nobody in particular.

He burst in with, 'Look! This was under the tree. My Spy-tortoise found it. It's addressed to me and Beth, and it's marked urgent!'

'*Do* be careful!' said his mother, straightaway spraying clouds of 'Instant Sterility Plus' and hurriedly covering the table with a thick cloth.

'No jokes?' said Beth, coughing through the spray.

'No jokes,' said Joe. 'Really.'

'A gift from the gods, then – well, the poor ones, anyway. Let's open it.'

Beth cut the string and lifted the cardboard lid.

Four pairs of eyes strained to see what was inside. Copurrnicus was watching from Joe's shoulder.

'Lots of old newspaper,' said Beth as she threw the first layer onto the floor.

Joe couldn't resist pulling out a few handfuls as well, and it was he who first caught sight of a hidden object: a curved piece of silver.

'Found something!' said Joe. 'Over to you.'

When Beth had finished the unpacking, she lifted out a silver bird about the size of a pigeon. Its eyes were pale blue and had the strange effect of looking straight at you wherever you went. For a moment everyone was quiet, even their mother. The beauty of the bird was so striking that silence was the only possible response. Beth was the first to say what the others were thinking: 'It's incredible! Totally, really beautiful.'

Joe said nothing, but he was fascinated by the bird's appearance. He also noticed that, when she held it up for all to see, Beth's face glowed. Reflected daylight from the window? There was no way that light could be coming from the bird itself, was there?

'How *gorgeous*, darling! What a *marvellous* gift!' said her mother, finding her voice again. 'I have never seen anything like it. Let's put it on the cupboard to catch the sun.'

Beth, enchanted by the bird, was in no hurry to put it anywhere. 'It's silver,' she said, 'but I can see rainbow colours move across it like a wave.' Then, without altogether believing it: 'Sometimes I can see right through it.'

'I know how that's done,' said Joe. 'It's a shiny metal with microscopic lines to make a diffraction grating. That would cause colours that move. And you can see through metal if it's very thin.'

She stroked it. 'It feels warm, like it's covered with real feathers,' added Beth in surprise.

'It must…' said Joe, '…have another layer on top… etched in a different way…' He was finding it difficult to think how that could happen. 'Or…' His voice faded.

Beth, absorbed by the gentle feel and shimmering beauty of her present, let Joe's theories float past without comment.

'Who sent it?' asked Mother. 'I can't think of anyone we know who breeds pigeons, especially silver ones. Aunt Flo's husband, Dennis, dabbled in that sort of thing once, but he died ages ago. He had severe Bird Fancier's Lung. Quite unusual. She never kept any animals after that. As I was saying to Mrs Dimworthy, birds are—'

'Let's look in the box again,' interrupted Joe. 'It was addressed to me as well.'

Beth rested the bird on the silver, branch-shaped stand that came with it and tipped the box upside down. More paper poured into the paws of the playful Copurrnicus, then two other objects fell out: something flat and brown that slipped onto the floor, and an envelope with Beth's name on it.

Quick-eyed Joe dived under the table. There he spotted a newspaper with the headline 'The King's Madness – Latest'. It reminded him of when his class

6

at school gave their teacher a set of pens filled with disappearing ink. Mr King went screaming bonkers after writing reports all day only to find he was left with a pile of blank pages. What else was there to find?

Beth opened her envelope and took out a card. On the front was a drawing of her bird, though it was flying through clouds rather than sitting on its stand. She read it out loud:

Dear Beth,

Can you and Joe rescue us? We are under a curse.

No one knows where it comes from and no one can unbind it.

Together, you have what we need.

If you are willing to help, change into a servant beyond the clock.

I hope you like the silver bird. He's called Thyripolis.

I will explain when we meet.

Please come!

Granelda

'Who's Granelda?' asked Beth. 'And what does all *that* mean? It sounds terrible! And why has she sent me a silver bird?'

'I really don't know,' said Mother. 'I thought *you* might have an answer – she seems to know you. You did have a Great Aunt Ethel once, but she never learnt to write, so it can't be her. Then again, our second cousin, Bert – the one with the red hair—'

'Sounds like a very old lady to me,' said Joe, appearing above the table. 'Here's *my* parcel.' He showed off a small, flat package with his name on it, written in the same hand as the card.

'Strange…' said Beth. 'Do open it. Here, have my scissors.'

Out of the crinkled brown paper tumbled a thin, old-fashioned book with dark green covers decorated in gold. Its fancy lettering announced:

JOE RAVEN
A PERSONAL GUIDE

He looked inside and read aloud the opening page:

Dear Joe
    I so hope you and Beth can help us.
    Keep this with you. It will keep you alive.
    Like Beth, start beyond the clock.
    Take the finest costume – you will look good!
    Please bring your amazing OAK. No one here has that sort of magic.
    Travel well.
    Granelda

'Granelda!' said Joe. 'Who *is* Granelda? She even knows about my OAK!'

'Which is?' asked Beth.

'My Outside Adventure Kit – all my best gadgets for exploring, in a waterproof pouch.'

'Keep reading,' said his mother. 'You've got such a *lovely* voice.'

But as Joe turned over the pages, his face changed from excited to puzzled to disappointed. 'There is nothing in it!' he said. 'It's empty! How can that be a "Personal Guide"?! Blank pages will keep me alive, will they?'

'Perhaps it's a notebook for your travels,' offered Beth.

'To see the mysterious Granelda? Perhaps not.'

'But she's asked us to rescue people who are under a curse. She seems to think we can.'

'How can we meet her when we don't even know who or where she is? Anyway, I don't believe in curses. We're in the twenty-first century, right?'

'Never mind,' said Mother. 'I'll ask my cousin, Alf. He lives in Wimblesweed and is *very* good at crosswords. Now, my darlings...' She stood up. 'I've a beautiful surprise for you! Today we are going to visit Boar Hall in its *wonderful* gardens designed by Capability Brown. You'll love it. The morning is for you to explore, then we'll have a *feast* in the Servants' Quarters. After that, a *wonderful* play-time before we visit the shop!'

Joe's cloud of disappointment turned stormy. Not only had he planned that morning to explode hydrogen bubbles with high-energy sparks, but he had also been sent a new code to decipher from his friend, Cy. He was not expecting to go out. He did not want to go out. Could he write in his so-called *Guide* about visiting

Boar Hall? Yes, he could! 'The First Golden Rule of Travel: Avoid *boring* places.' Some unknown 'Granelda' wanting him to carry round an empty book all day to find a 'curse' was rubbish! He could stay alive without it, thank you. What sort of help could she possibly expect?

Beth was looking eye to eye with Thyripolis. Then, as though someone had posted it into her mind, she saw a picture of Joe falling down an endless dark hole in the ground. Seeping out of it was the faint smell of the sea. Somehow, she knew that Joe's fall wasn't an accident, but he was still in danger. He was trying to find something... some... She blinked. Thyripolis was still staring at her, but the picture and the sea smell had gone. She knew she must speak to Joe – not about the deep hole but about going to Boar Hall. He *must* come. The gifts, the card, this picture and the outing... they must all be connected...

She tried some possible bait: 'We'll have pancakes at lunch time,' and, 'There's an old science exhibition where you can make things work.'

'I can make more interesting things work *here*. Who wants old?'

Beth sighed. 'Look at what Granelda's written, Joe.'

He read Beth's card for himself and, again, the writing in his *Guide*. Then he smiled. 'I know. *You* wrote these! Like your plays. *You're* Granelda. You set this up for my Spy-tortoise to find. Great idea, thanks.'

'Whoa! I didn't even know about your tortoise till you showed me. And I don't know how the parcel got there – it's a mystery. But we've both got messages asking for our help.'

'Delivered in a cardboard box from nowhere... It's got to be a hoax.'

'With presents like that inside? Maybe this "Granelda" will meet us at Boar Hall. She seems to know we're travelling, and she's heard about your gadgets. Let's go there and see!'

Joe was bothered. Very bothered. There was too much he couldn't explain. Where *did* the box come from? Thy-whatever was weirdly beautiful, but it couldn't really be like Beth said. Her theatrical imagination again. But, how could 'Granelda' write about his OAK when he'd never told anyone about it?

'Do you think Granelda is real?' he asked Beth in a flat voice, guessing her answer.

'Yes. I do. I think all this is real and that we can't just stay here and ignore her.'

Joe grunted, clenched his teeth and retreated to his Creatory. He stared out of his window at the tree where the box had landed. Maybe his father did leave it there as a brain teaser, but to ask him was out of the question. His garden office was out of bounds and disturbing him would cause an explosion. His thoughts jumped up and down like puppies snapping at his logic. With a swirling mind and considerable effort, he was just able to imagine that Granelda could be real. If so, her words were clues. She and others were in danger and they needed his help. His inventions would make it possible.

Suddenly, curiously, he felt proud. Could his OAK *really* be essential to the success of a rescue mission? It did hold some of his best gadgets: his Energy Alert Responder (EAR) that sensed every type of invisible force field; a pocket-sized Omniscope to see everything from microscopic particles to distant planets in the sharpest detail; and, best of all, his PEST – a Pan-Electromagnetic Spectrum Torch – that produced X-rays, light of all kinds and radio waves as well as high-energy lasers.

His jangling thoughts calmed down. An idea crystallised in his brain: *Let's put Granelda to the test – follow her clues and see if she appears. At least that will save us being deadly bored at Boar Hall.*

'Going now, children!'

Their mother's voice filled every room in the house. Joe commanded, 'All Off!' to his power supplies, reset the CREAM and headed for the car.

Beth gave a long look at Thyripolis before joining the others. His eyes seemed particularly bright, but her thoughts, surprisingly, framed a clear picture of Joe's book. When she had climbed into her seat she asked if he had brought it.

'No!' said Joe. 'Why would I? It didn't say much, and I have got my OAK.'

'Do take it! It might still be useful.' She made no mention of her prompt from Thyripolis.

As the challenge of looking for Granelda took shape in his mind, Joe's black clouds lightened. He hurried back for the *Guide*.

Before he left the kitchen, he looked around: Copurrnicus was flopped contentedly in a patch of sunshine. The bird? The silver bird... was missing. Joe stared rigidly at the empty stand, then darted round the room, eyes flitting everywhere. No joy. Nowhere to be seen. Half his brain shouted for him to run and tell Beth at once. The other half reasoned that the bird must be somewhere nearby – perhaps put behind the cupboard for safe-keeping? The doors and windows were closed. His father had fixed thirteen burglar alarms downstairs and nine upstairs, all wired to his garden office, so the chances of it being stolen were tiny. Best say nothing to Beth now but find the bird when they came home.

Guide in hand, Joe ran back to join the others. In his head he was ready. He and Beth had been presented with a challenge to save lives – whatever the 'curse' turned out to be. And his inventions would be the answer. Assuming Granelda was real.

CHAPTER 2

A QUARTER PAST ONE

Two towering iron gates guarded the entrance to Boar Hall, each carrying the blue and golden crest of its owner, the Ninth Duke of Curdlingshire. Beyond lay a long, winding driveway lined from beginning to end with dark, mottled statues. They were not of warriors and noblemen but of ordinary tradesmen and merchants, even complete families. Only a few were standing tall and proud. Most looked crushed by fear or pain.

'Why do they look so miserable?' asked Beth as they drove past.

'Because they're really bored?' suggested Joe, looking up for a moment from sorting out his OAK.

'You'd look glum if you were stuck out there in all weathers with pigeons landing on your head,' said their mother. 'You could easily get arthritis, never mind pneumonia. One night, my cousin Bert nearly turned into to a statue while he was guarding Edinburgh Castle all alone. He's been as stiff as a board ever since—'

'*Watch out!*' shouted Beth.

Mother swerved sharply to avoid hitting a small, well-dressed lady striding towards the courtyard. When everyone had disembarked, she hugged her children tightly and, with a cheer-leader's voice and beaming smile, bellowed, 'Here begins our *Day of Delight!*'

Two birds took flight, Beth winced and Joe tried to become invisible. Fortunately, the selfie she tried to take recorded only the pink feather on the top of her summer hat. In a quieter voice, his mother gave him a meaningful look. She reminded him of a local jingle: '*A day at Boar Hall is no bore at all!*'

The neat lady with tight curls and a clipboard appeared at the top of the steps to the Duke's Family Entrance. She stood in front of its dark oak doors to make ready for her guided tour. On either side of her stood enormous statues of snarling dogs. A boar's head with fierce tusks glared from the archway above.

In a thin voice she began: 'My name is Millicent Mildew. Welcome to Boar Hall!

'This magnificent building was created in 1688 by a nobleman called "The Proud Duke". Later, it fell into the line of the Dukes of Curdlingshire. It didn't actually *fall*, of course; *they* moved into *it*… one at a time, you see.' The lady nearly laughed. Joe yawned. The other visitors looked like statues.

Miss Mildew continued: 'Behind these doors are the Duke's Private Apartments, and today you are allowed to explore them *on your own!*' She sounded like a teacher giving sweets to children who didn't deserve them.

'Beyond the family rooms is the Grand Enlightening Theatre, created for demonstrating the latest scientific marvels of the time: experiments with static electricity. Visitors were shocked right out of their seats by an electrical wind propelled by *thousands* of volts!'

Miss Mildew's audience were unmoved. Mother shared with a random bystander the tragic story of her brother who died taking bread out of a live electric toaster with his fork.

As the guide warbled on, the attention of the Ravens wandered. Joe was checking his PEST; Beth, with a faraway smile, was thinking of Thyripolis and his silvery feathers glowing in the sun; and their mother was desperately looking for signs to the nearest café. Miss Mildew's enthusiastic sentences continued with list of things to explore:

'...a secret tunnel linking the main house to the Servants' Quarters.'

'...a massive display of rare scientific instruments belonging to King George III.'

'...the ruins of the Spykeeper's Fortress at the river mouth downstream.'

'...a remarkable grandfather clock on the main staircase that has never stopped since the house was built.'

And, '...a boat trip to the medieval town of Caladrin with its high citadel – the Duke's official seat.'

While not listening to Miss Mildew, Joe studied a nearby round bell-tower covered in old ivy. Perhaps he could climb it – on the far side, of course, out of view – then trigger the bell mechanism to see what the staff and visitors did next. His getaway would be through the trees behind.

Beth, who had followed his gaze, suddenly spotted a brilliant silver light on the edge of the bell-chamber. Almost at once, it darted across the courtyard, passing low over her head. It scattered rainbow colours as it went then disappeared under the eaves of the Servants' Quarters. Beth stared hard at where it had vanished, hoping that it would reappear – but in vain.

'Did you see that, Joe?' she said.

'What?'

'A bright light flying from the bell-tower to the roof over there.' She pointed to where it had disappeared. 'It came really close.'

'No.'

'Are you sure?'

'Yes.'

'That's odd. You were looking exactly where I was.'

Joe's brain cells found no easy answer.

Beth voiced a thought: 'I wonder... do you think it could be—'

'...difficult to explain?' interrupted Joe, worrying that the conversation could take a difficult turn. 'It *could*... But it's probably the angle of the sun... or... because there's steam coming out of that pipe in the wall.'

Beth looked doubtful. Joe looked quickly at the tower and said no more.

'Joe…' asked Beth, '…was my silver bird all right when you went back to the house?'

Joe's stomach hit ground level.

'Coffee! We *must* get to the café for drinks! And how about a *maple syrup pancake* to start the day? You can have it with *piles* of ice cream, darlings.'

For once, the interruption of his mother's ear-rattling voice proved a rescue not a disaster.

'Yes, sure!' he said, hoping this would seem to answer Beth's question as well.

As they headed for the Servants' Hall, Beth kept looking for the mysterious light. So did Joe, without showing it. Over coffee, their mother discovered an old friend and within seconds burst into a long description of yet another strange member of her sprawling family tree. Joe and Beth, cheerfully full of unhealthy snacks and drinks, were soon dismissed with, 'Explore what you like and have fun – but be back here for lunch at a quarter past one.'

As they wandered down the long corridor of the Servants' Quarters Joe asked, 'Why then?'

Beth was on stage again: 'Cherished sibling, the Web of Time disposes the hours of our lives. Perhaps a Spirit of Feasting has cast her spell upon that special moment to crown the endeavours of the culinary slaves for our delectation.'

'What?'

'I've no idea. Random activity of Mother's brain?'

'Let's try to find Granelda before lunch,' said Joe.

'Find Granelda? You don't believe she exists.'

'...maybe not, but we *could* see if she does... I've planned an anti-boredom project called "DIGITAL".'

'Digital?'

'A mission to Decide If Granelda Is Truly ALive.'

'So how do we do that, Mr Puzzle-Brain?'

'Suppose Granelda knows not only that we are going out but that we are visiting Boar Hall—'

'How could she do that?'

'...Haven't worked that out yet... But she could be here—'

'It's an enormous place—' said Beth.

'...and we don't know what she looks like.'

'What about the clues in your *Guide*?'

Joe had not made friends with his *Guide*, but he pulled it out and read the opening page again. 'Nothing about finding Granelda, just about me taking my OAK and looking good in "the finest costume". Are you sure you didn't write this?'

'No, and *no!*'

'Did you bring Granelda's card?'

'Left it at home.'

Close to his sister's nose, Joe pulled a strange face.

'But I do know the words by heart.'

'So...?'

'The only possible clue was about changing into "a servant beyond the clock".'

'We're in the right place for servants,' said Joe. 'I've seen them in fancy dress going in and out of that room.'

He nodded towards a doorway further down the corridor. 'Worth an inspection?'

Beth agreed.

Getting close, they saw that the doorway led to the Pantry and the Great Kitchen.

'Look!' said Beth. 'A large clock on the wall of that staircase next to the door. This must be it. I'll try to find out how to become a servant from the kitchen staff.'

'One of *them* could be Granelda,' suggested Joe. 'Perhaps she's in charge?'

Inside the pantry, the worktops and shelves were covered with tasty-looking food. In spite of mission DIGITAL, temptation drew Joe to a display of freshly made treacle tarts, then whispered excellent reasons for him to try one out. Dawdling behind, and with no visitors around, he made quick work of the first crunchy bite. A moment later a sound like 'Yerch!' squeezed out through a powdery mush in his mouth. The tart was made of Plaster-of-Paris. It stuck in his teeth with an awful taste, and the powder had scattered all over the worktop and floor. Overcome by the horror of being caught, the sound of approaching footsteps left him no option but to flee the mess in a hurry. He slid into the Great Kitchen, spitting fragments of mock treacle tart into a fire bucket, desperately hoping that no one would notice.

Beth had been watching several older girls dressed as maids and cooks from long ago. Two were stirring bright yellow ice cream; one was stoking the fire. Another, polishing large copper saucepans, stopped to complain about the chores that filled a servant's sixteen-hour day before she could go to a freezing bed in a tiny attic. Beth asked her how she could get a servant's job.

'Do you mean if you were in the eighteenth century or if you wanted to act the part like us?' she answered.

'To act the part.'

'Great! You'll need to ask at the office in the main building. There's a waiting list, though. It's very popular.'

'No chance to start today, then?'

'It usually takes a few months.'

'Oh… Thanks… Do you know anybody here called Granelda?'

The servant girl shook her head.

As Beth moved away to find Joe, the girl called out, 'If you want to dress like a servant today, you could try the main house. There's some old costumes there for visitors.'

'Where?'

'Up the main staircase, I think.'

All this time, Joe had become interested the workings of the spit and roasting machinery of the enormous central fireplace. Its vertical hooks and rods looked to be rotated by gears on a shaft going to a small room behind. Mr Curious-Fingers wandered on to explore. Levers and handles beckoned. Activating a green button labelled 'UP' proved irresistible. *Click*. A grinding sound began. Pulleys with chains started to revolve.

Almost at once, squeals and cries of alarm came from the kitchen. Fuelled by guilty fear, Joe leapt to press the red switch for 'DOWN', only to hear a crash, followed by a gasp from a group of visitors. One of the roasting hooks had caught in the ties of a maid's apron. It had lifted her high in the air, spinning her round before plunging her down hard onto the grate. Red-faced, he rushed out to say sorry – straight into the very large stomach of a Boar Hall attendant. Angry shouting burst from the purple face above it, followed by deep apologies from Joe, sisterly support from Beth and first aid for the fallen maid. After the painful eviction of both Raven children from the Servants' Quarters they ran across the courtyard and disappeared into Boar Hall to search for the main staircase. 'It's the other side of the exhibition,' said an attendant. 'You'll have to go through there.'

In the enormous gallery further on, a glow from yellow-flamed oil lamps spread over the exhibits of old scientific equipment. Glass tubes sparked like lightning from static electricity stored in 'Leyden jars'. Joe couldn't help trying the handle of a machine built around a large glass disc with silver segments. Spinning it fast made his hair stand on end like needles. Suddenly, he was tormented by a sharp, high-pitched noise. What was *that*? Security alarm? Ruined ears? *Ears. That's it!* He tracked the sound to the EAR in his pocket. It had been triggered by the machine's electric charge. A switch to 'MUTE' made it silent.

While Joe was being electrified, Beth had wandered off to explore racks of leather-bound books in an old library. She was interrupted by low, cooing noise that made her look up. Her skin shrank and tingled. Her face lit up. Her heart pounded. She stared, utterly wide-eyed. Thyripolis was standing on a pile of books shining with warmth. She wanted to him pick him up and stroke him, but for some reason, the time did not seem right. She thought she saw him blink. Then he turned his head. He was alive! He had flown from home and found her. She gazed at him, taking in every detail…

The silver bird nodded towards an old brown book on the table in front of her. She glanced down, then slowly read in the depth of his eyes that she should read the open page. It showed a drawing of two men standing, each holding an archery bow. They looked very much the same, except that one was much rounder than the other. There was one other difference, too: the larger man looked pleased. *Pleased with himself*, thought Beth, looking closely. The other man looked bewildered and sad.

A caption underneath the picture was headlined '*Remarkable Victory for Lord Tresquin*'. Under that it continued: 'On the seventeenth day of June 1774, against all expectations, Lord Castus was defeated by his twin to become the Fifth Duke of Curdlingshire. Lord Tresquin paid tribute to his brother, well known as the best archer in England. The new Duke recognised that the contest could easily have ended the other way and thanked the National Archery Field Captain for his impartial judgement of the event.'

Beth looked up towards Thyripolis to find an explanation, as well as simply to delight in looking at him again. He was out of focus. She blinked hard and looked again. He was even more blurred and his eyes had become dull. Gradually, he was evaporating into a fine silver mist that was getting thinner as it grew. Soon, he had vanished completely.

A cold pain wrapped round her. Her head shouted, *Why?* Her eyes began to prickle. 'He came to show me something that must be important.' She drew in a quick breath. 'I don't understand. Please come back, Thyripolis, *please!*' She couldn't help saying this out loud, though there was no one to hear her. She waited, but all stayed quiet except for the distant sound of an old steam engine. In the silence she began to notice a strange smell. From the engine? No, much more unusual – like a rainbow of scents: the sharpness of lemon, the sweetness of toffee, the freshness of a pine forest, the wideness of the sea, the warmth of a log fire. She couldn't describe all these at the time, nor decide where they came from. Their effect was exciting and calming at the same time. She looked at the picture again. What was she supposed to learn from it? Should she tell Joe what she had seen? Perhaps not. He'd just find some clever reason why she was imagining it all. Maybe Thyripolis would appear again... The rainbow scents lingered until Beth met Joe again by an old model globe. Her watch squeaked that it was one o'clock. Knowing nods were exchanged and the pair hurried to the main hall.

The grand staircase was right in front of them with a high, shiny handrail and a faded carpet. After climbing the wide steps to a short landing, they were confronted by the tallest and most ornate grandfather clock ever seen. Surely, this must be the clock of Granelda's clue.

'Beyond the clock…' Beth quoted.

Several steps higher and around a corner, they found another landing with a window. Joe stopped to look out. In the distance he could see the remains of what was the 'Spykeeper's Fortress'.

'I wonder who crashed that to the ground? Not much left.'

'Come on! We're running out of time.'

A few paces further on they reached a store of old costumes in a chest. A hanging rail and a mirror stood nearby.

'We're here!' said Beth. 'This is it. A servant for me and a fine costume for you, lucky thing.'

Grunt.

Straightaway, Beth began sorting through the collection. How much she preferred her first find – an elegant silk gown with golden trimmings – but, following Granelda's instructions, she sought out the blue-grey linen dress and top of a scullery maid. 'Oh, well…' she whispered. 'Now to play a servant – without a script…' Behind an ancient ornamental screen she exchanged her coat for her costume. It was far more difficult to put on than she was expecting – tight and ticklish. And it smelt old. By the time she had finished, her head felt pinched and her feet swollen.

'Your turn, Joe. Come and find your "finest costume". There's not much to choose from.'

Instantly Joe felt a million miles away from his comfort zone. *Dressing up* – really? *Does our mission have to be* this *embarrassing?* 'Stick with the instructions,' he kept repeating to himself, still wondering whatever this had to do with finding Granelda. Hidden behind the screen, he took a deep breath and hung up his jacket. He grabbed a smart, long-tailed brown coat labelled '*As worn by a successful merchant*'. It fitted him well but felt surprisingly cold. He couldn't help a sudden shiver, and for a moment, he felt squeezed sharply all over. That would do. Just the jacket. No more.

They stopped to look at each other.

'I've done it!' said Joe with a look of having just completed a double marathon in half the usual time. His achievement was rewarded with Beth's wide look of surprise and delight.

'That's amazing!' she said. 'I didn't think you'd bother to put on breeches with a shirt and waistcoat. And,' as she looked down, 'stockings as well. And *shoes*. I didn't even see those under the rack. That's fantastic!'

'Nice joke, Beth, though I did manage to put on the coat without running away.'

'But you're wearing the whole costume.'

Joe looked at Beth with an odd expression. 'No, I'm *not*. Fermented maple syrup. Must have made your head squidgy.'

'Yes, you *are*. Look in the mirror!'

Joe stared at his reflection and went rigid with disbelief. The boy he saw was fully dressed as a merchant's son from ages ago – and it was him. His stomach tightened. His brain cells fizzed. Maybe it wasn't really a mirror but a screen with a smart digital image... DIGITAL... *The mission... Granelda... Did she plan this?*

Beth looked over his shoulder and her reflection caught Joe's eye.

'Hey, what about you? Where did you get your frilly cap and apron? And *you've* got shiny shoes on, too. Look!'

'What!' cried Beth, seeing herself exactly as Joe described. 'How could that happen?'

There was no doubt that both children were fully dressed in eighteenth-century costumes. They stared silently at each other, heads crowded with thoughts but empty of explanations.

'We've done what "Granelda" wanted and we haven't met her.' Beth decided this was enough. With a gnawing fear, she suggested, 'Let's change back and get lunch... We're late already.'

'Sure! Straightaway. I said it was a hoax.'

But the rail holding their own clothes had vanished. There was no sign of the chest. The mirror and the screen had disappeared too. Beth spotted that the carpet was no longer faded and that the pictures on the walls had changed.

'What's going on?' she squeezed out from a dry throat.

'Time travel,' said Joe calmly.

The grandfather clock gave single chime. It was a quarter past one, but two hundred years in the past.

CHAPTER 3

HOUNDED

'I thought time travel would be much more exciting,' said Joe. 'High-energy atomic reconfiguration, flashes of all the years in between, a force of clashing energies… not just slipping into fancy dress. At least it wasn't a caveman's outfit.'

Beth wasn't listening. She was looking round, trying to work out what age they were in. 'It looks like we're Georgians, late Georgians,' she said.

'I thought we were on time—'

'Ha!'

'Will we have to speak Georgian?'

'No, Mr Scientist. Georgian-speak was the same as ours.' An idea clicked: 'Did you look at the newspaper that came with our presents?'

'Under the table I did.'

'And?'

'D-*rab*! Small, crowded print in thin columns. No pictures. Something about a king being mad that reminded me of—'

'George III! He had an illness that made him insane. You didn't see the date, did you?

'No.'

'But if Granelda's wrapping paper came from the eighteenth century—'

'…she could be here too—'

'…and we've been brought to find her.'

'DIGITAL positive – nearly.'

'Right. But…' Beth's fears suddenly welled up again. 'What do we do now? We'll soon be spotted. Who do we say we are? How do we explain why we're here?'

'We're *us*, great actress. You're a servant and I'm a merchant's son. We're looking for our aunt Granelda. How about lunch? It's gone a quarter past one. Dressed like that you might get one free in the Servants' Hall.'

'And then be forced to slave away for hours in—'

'Hey! Must look at that!' Passing the window, Joe had seen that the Spykeeper's Fortress was no longer in ruins. 'I'll use my Omniscope on *Distance Hi Mag* to get a really close…' As a black cloud invaded his thoughts, his voice faded away.

'What?'

'My Omniscope. It's gone! It was part of the OAK in my coat pocket – the one that's now stuck in the future.'

'Maybe it's in the pocket of your coat now?' *Where did that idea come from?*

'Yes, Beth. I did make it to go anywhere... Perhaps not any*when*.'

'You could still look.'

Grunt.

Though his sister being right was always a pain, discovering his OAK in the large pocket of his merchant's coat switched on his sunshine. Finding the *Guide* sent by a mysterious old lady did not. He gave it to Beth while he checked out his inventions.

Grabbing his Omniscope, he then lined it up for a sharp view of the fortress. Cannons were mounted all along its crenelated walls and towers. He could see at least a dozen soldiers in full battle dress, all carrying muskets.

While waiting for Joe, Beth flipped through the pages of his *Guide*. Then: 'Joe! You've been writing in your book.'

'Really? I don't remember that.' He stayed focused on the fortress. 'Maybe my hands crept into my pocket and scribbled something secretly on the way to Boar Hall. What did I write?'

'The numbers nought to nine and the alphabet, all set out in neat rows.'

'No,' said Joe, 'not my style. Did *you* write them?' ... Probably not,' he added quickly, ducking to avoid a flying 'No!'. 'Then, QED, it must be magic – a mysterious agent generating interesting characters.'

While he put the Omniscope away, his brain

juggled with some non-magical ideas. 'Are all the letters the same?'

'No, they're all different – as usual. You can make a lot more words that way.'

'Silly! I wondered if any of them had tiny changes or marks that could give us a coded message,' he added.

Beth peered hard at the page but saw nothing unusual.

Joe burst across her view. 'Let's use this.' He reset his Omniscope to *Close-up Hi Mag* and scanned the page methodically. All stayed quiet, except for the noisy tick of the grandfather clock.

'Found something!' said Joe. 'All the characters have a small dotted pattern inside, but five have numbers instead. The 4 is labelled 1, the G is 2, the C is 3, the U is 4 and the V is 5. So, in that order: *4-G-C-U-V*.' That's the answer.'

'The answer to what? I can't see what it means,' said Beth.

'I'm working on it.'

'Say it out loud again,' said Beth.

'4-G-C-U-V.' Joe was pleased to have a code to solve, but where could he start with this one?

'When you say it out loud,' said Beth, 'it sounds like, "For G see UV."'

'That's what I said!'

'No, I mean that if we want to find G then we need to look at UV – whatever G, U and V are.'

Joe, miffed that Beth had come up with another bright idea, nevertheless sparked in with: 'In my world,

UV means ultraviolet light. Perhaps we have to look *with* it rather than look *at* it… Hey! My PEST can generate UV light!'

'So, that just leaves us with the mysterious G. The mysterious…'

'*Granelda!*' they said at the same time.

'We *will* be meeting her today!' said Beth, bright-eyed. 'We just need your UV light to find her!'

'You mean UV light makes the mysterious Granelda glow in the dark? That's useful. Any particularly dark spot round here you suggest we look into?'

'Stop being unhelpful! This is getting exciting! What else could we shine it on?'

Footsteps and voices from below interrupted their conversation. Beth and Joe moved sharply and silently away from the bannister to a corner by the clock. Whoever they were downstairs went away again, though Beth then heard a scratching noise from the landing above. She was about to tell Joe about it when…

'Ouch!' she cried. 'That's hot! The *Guide* is burning me up.'

'Perhaps it's trying to tell you something,' said Joe, resigning himself to yet another mad happening.

The distraction of the hot book meant that neither Joe nor Beth saw Thyripolis sitting on top of the clock. At the same time, an idea sprang into Beth's mind. 'Shine it on the same page.'

'Hmm. Why not? Maybe it'll surprise us by turning into a pizza. I'm starving!'

In the shade of the clock. Joe grabbed his PEST, set

it to *UV300:100:150* and switched it on. By then, the *Guide* had cooled down enough to rest on Beth's hand. In the shade of the clock they stared hard at its pages. The paper and grey characters stayed dull, but other writing appeared, glowing brilliantly in green: '3 *Quince Cottages*'.

'Solved! We'll find Granelda at Quince Cottages,' whispered Beth.

'Wherever *they* are,' said Joe, feeling much more like lunch than searching for an old lady in a frilly cottage. And his sister had guessed the answer again...

'Does the *Guide* give any—'

A stomach-curdling growl cut Beth short. Should they stay hidden or move? Joe's curiosity won. The time travellers moved briskly to the landing to see where it came from. At the top of the next flight of stairs above them was a terrifying, real-life hound, like one of the stone dogs they had seen next to Millicent Mildew. It glared at them through red eyes, saliva dripping from its open mouth. Four finely sharpened fangs were set into its powerful jaws. On seeing them, it let out an eerie howl. Joe stood motionless. He stretched his neck forward and stared angrily into the dog's eyes. Beth moved back. The dog barked sharply and moved one step down. Joe made no move at all. The growling started again, softly at first but getting louder as the dog advanced further down the stairs. Joe leant forward, hardly blinking and not for a second losing eye contact with the hound.

In a quiet voice he spoke to his PEST, setting it to

6K Strobe:75:25. The dog tilted his head on one side as it crouched down, ready to jump and tear at any flesh it could reach. Joe leant further forwards.

'Don't get so close, Joe. *Don't!*' pleaded Beth, not minding if anyone could hear her.

Joe took no notice. He stepped onto the first stair. Beth mouthed a silent, '*No!*'

After a moment of an intense stalemate, Joe whispered, 'Strobe and go!' Then with critical timing, he pressed 'FIRE'. A vivid, flashing beam hit the dog full on. Its face twisted horribly. The hound collapsed, convulsed wildly and then tumbled down the stairs in front of him.

'Now!' said Joe in a loud whisper. 'Go!'

The Ravens ran down to the main hall and turned left into a wide, empty corridor.

Statues were everywhere. So were bowls of wavy green plants with enormous leaves. No one was in sight. They paused for breath, each with their mind racing to think of what to do next.

Beth caught sight of a portrait hanging on a nearby wall. It sprang her memory back to the page that Thyripolis showed her in the old library. The larger man was still looking pleased with himself, but he was no longer holding his bow. This was now shown in the background, resting on an archery target where three arrows had all landed on the bullseye.

Joe was looking elsewhere. He found a newspaper on a low cupboard. He quickly scanned the front page. 'Look! Here's a date: Tuesday, March 10, 1789. It's all about George III recovering from his madness. He was about to return to—'

'*Hey, you!* What are you doing here?' An elderly butler had appeared from a nearby room carrying a tray of glasses. He was limping as though someone had just stamped on his foot, and he was furious.

'Run or stay?' whispered Beth.

'Let's try talking…' said Joe.

Beth rated that a bad idea but went along with it.

The heavy-breathing butler came closer. 'You! Servant girl. Why aren't you emptying the chamber pots in the second-floor bedrooms?'

'Please, Sir, I was asked to clean the leaves of the aspidistra plants down here instead.'

'And who told you to do that?'

'The housekeeper, Sir.'

'Really? Really, indeed? We don't have any plants called "aspidistras".'

'Oh, I thought—'

'Anyway,' the butler continued, '*if* Mrs Bugle told you to do as you say – if she *really* did – then you've got the plant name wrong. These are *Columnifitendriata*.' He seemed rather pleased he could say that. He paused to let the information find its way into the dim servant's head. 'And where are your cleaning materials?'

'…I'm just looking for them, Sir. The head gardener said he had a special tincture for the leaves that he was going to let me use.'

'How unusual,' said the butler, giving Beth a long stare.

Did he believe this story? It didn't look like it.

He turned to Joe. 'And you, child? You look like you're from a swindling merchant's family.' His eyes narrowed. 'What's your excuse for being in Boar Hall?'

'Dog-training, Sir,' said Joe without hesitation. 'I've just been upstairs demonstrating a new amazing device we brought into the country this morning.'

'We?' The butler's eyebrows rose.

'I'm in a Company of Importers in Caladrin, Sir.' The adrenaline rush was doing wonders for Joe's imagination.

'Called…?' The eyebrows moved higher.

'Um… "Advanced Technology Techniques in Caladrin" – "ATTIC" for short.'

'Well…' The butler smiled kindly, except for his eyes. '*Very* good explanations by you both.'

Beth and Joe smiled back weakly, relieved if still painfully scared about what would happen next.

'But they are all *lies!*' the butler thundered. 'So, you had better come with me to the Lord Tresquin's Guard to see what he wants to do with you. We do have a small prison on site – rather cold and damp, I'm told. You're too young for the Well… He may prefer to give you hard labour. We are rather short-staffed.'

A fleeting glance between Joe and Beth triggered a rapid escape.

'Sorry – got an invitation for tea,' Joe shouted as they ran off at full speed down the corridor, leaving the butler stranded with his glasses.

They ran through a small hall into a parlour where

two well-dressed men were talking closely over tea. The Ravens' only option was to go forward, to the door opposite. They hurried across the room silently, bending down to avoid being noticed. Joe looked round to check out the tea party. Bad move. He bumped into a pedestal with a vase on top. It tilted over, banged on the floor and made a muddy mess on the carpet. The men looked up, then shouted. They gave chase at once, followed by the limping, wheezing butler, but Joe and Beth scrambled out of the door without being caught.

In the next room, a young woman was playing a spinet and singing opera in almost the same key. Beth and Joe skimmed past her without being seen, as did the three men in pursuit. After them, with silent and nimble paws, came the hound. It had recovered from Joe's flashing light and was on the scent for revenge. Taking the far exit from the music room, Joe and Beth turned into another wide corridor. There they spied a door with the sign 'Servants Only'.

'Let's go in there while everyone goes past,' she said. 'I'm a servant, after all.'

Joe nodded and tried the handle. 'Yes!' The door squeaked open.

Stepping quickly inside and closing it quietly, Joe turned the key in the lock and put it in his pocket. They were at the beginning of a long, narrow passageway with an uneven stone floor and a few windows along one wall. Several metres away, with its back to the other wall, stood a full coat of armour. It held a long-handled, medieval axe topped with a sharp, rounded blade.

'I guess he doesn't get much company down here,' said Joe.

As they came closer, they could hear the sound of creaking metal. The figure's head was turning slowly towards them. Its visor opened sharply to reveal a pair of widely staring eyes. The Ravens swallowed hard.

'Let's keep going steadily,' whispered Joe. 'We can't go back.'

Using both arms, the suit of armour began to raise its axe. With muscles that felt they were melting, Beth and Joe realised they had no choice but to go under it. They slowed their pace while trying furiously to think of a way out. At least the door to the corridor was locked, even if the men chasing them tried to come this way. Wrong! In the echoing silence, a faint click interrupted their thoughts. The lock! Someone following them had a key. *The bumbling butler*, guessed Joe. For a moment everything seemed to be happening in slow motion. Inside, bubbling brain cells fed a plan into his thinking.

'Listen, Beth. I can be *very* fast. As the blade reaches its highest point, I'll run under it. Tin Man looks like he hasn't got the quickest reactions in the world, so he probably won't drop the blade till I've got to the other side. You get ready to jump *over* the axe as soon as its blade hits the ground, before he can lift it up again. That'll fool him and we can get away. Yes?'

Beth nodded in agreement but with a terrible fear that this wouldn't work.

As the blade reached high in the air, Joe sprinted

forward. Beth stopped short of where she guessed the blade would fall, ready to jump when it did. Suddenly she let out a long, wild scream. Joe had tripped and was lying flat on the stone floor in line with the falling blade. Her mind shut off, she put her hands over her eyes and a loud rushing noise filled her head.

The blade fell with a deep, cracking thud. There was silence. Her voice could make no sound, but her whole body shrieked with horror. Then: 'Come on, Beth. *Jump!*'

The startling shout from Joe triggered her brain back into action. She stared at him, wide-eyed. He was lying in a tight curl round the feet of the armoured man. The blade had missed him completely. She jumped high over the axe and ran at speed beyond its reach. At the same time Joe uncurled himself and sprang to his feet. He gave a thumbs-up to metal man, telling him that he was wicked and should be ashamed. Then he dashed to join Beth. The man's eyes blinked and his visor fell shut. He struggled to lift the axe back to its 'on guard' position. It had got stuck in a crack between the stones of the floor.

'Brilliant move!' said Beth as they ran further along the passage.

Joe grinned. 'I guessed that if I rolled over to Mr Rusty's boots, the axe would be too long to reach me. Anyway, he wouldn't want to trim his toenails with that.'

Reaching the end of the passage, Beth and Joe faced a choice to turn right or left. By now, five people, as well as the bounding hound, had joined in the chase and were catching up at speed. A long curtain hung across the passageway to the right, so to stay out of view as long as possible, the Ravens pushed through it and ran on. The stone corridor in front of them was empty except for a large chest with short legs resting next to the wall halfway down.

'Why don't we hide in there?' said Beth. Joe agreed.

They reached the chest without being seen, but it took the two of them to lift up its heavy oak lid.

'Right!' said Joe. 'Rescue pod at the ready. Everybody in!'

There was just enough room for them both. Darkness and a raw, musty smell surrounded them.

'Let's give our friends something else to occupy them,' whispered Joe.

'Do we need to?'

No answer.

Joe, by feel, extracted his PEST again. This time he selected: *IR laser:35:5*. Beth helped push up the lid of the trunk just enough for him to point the laser beam at the curtain. FIRE! Within seconds, its material scorched and started smoking. A small flame erupted and quickly spread upwards.

Beth was troubled: 'Did you have to do that?'

'Don't worry. They'll just feel the chase heating up. It'll be all right. We're well hidden here.'

But unseen by the Ravens, the hound, still hunting for tasty pieces of Joe, pushed through the curtain and scampered briskly down the corridor towards its prey.

It had easily sniffed out where they were hiding. At the trunk it began howling, then jumping high and pawing at the wood. The commotion was noticed at once by the men in pursuit, one of whom was already intent on dealing severely with the young intruders. Carrying a thick cane, he left the others to fight the fire while he ran to the trunk. He tried to open the lid, but it moved only a little before it snapped shut again on his fingers. Roaring with pain and rage, he shook his arm in the air. Then, summoning a furious burst of energy, he flung the lid wide open – and froze. The trunk was empty.

CHAPTER 4

FINDING QUINCE COTTAGES

Inside the trunk, Beth and Joe knew that the hound's fury would lead to their capture. There was no way out. The strobe light could have fended off the dog again, but the party of men closing in on them meant their journey to find Quince Cottages was over. None of Joe's gadgets could make them invisible or change them temporarily into folded blankets. Curiously, he felt sorry that he would not meet Granelda after all. Beth knew enough history to picture what painful punishments could await them. They shrank into the darkness and tried to stop thinking. Their failure hurt. So much for a grand rescue mission!

As the howling of the hound grew louder, they had tried to move away from it by pushing themselves backwards. What came next was a complete surprise. The back of the trunk flapped down behind them while the false floor on which they had been sitting flipped up to take its place. As a result, Beth and Joe were propelled through a hole in the wall and dropped onto something soft. They were in a dim, echoing room, tangled up with each other on a straw mattress. Beth held a finger up to her mouth to stop Joe talking. They had no idea where they were or if anyone was nearby.

Muffled voices of bewilderment and anger tumbled down from the trunk. A loud banging on its sides followed as their foiled captors checked its walls and floor. Yes, they were all solid oak and didn't move. 'It's all clear underneath, too,' reported one of the men.

Having lost the scent, the growling dog quietened down and in a short time, the noise of fury and defeated footsteps faded away.

The round stone chamber into which Beth and Joe had fallen was lit by two narrow windows. It had no door, but steep spiral steps led downward from its wooden floor. A second flight rose up between the ceiling timbers to a chamber above. After the darkness of the trunk, they could easily see that the room was empty of people but full of dusty objects.

'We'd better get going to Quince Cottages,' said Beth. 'We might still be caught.'

Joe nodded. 'Which way – up or down?'

'I'll check the route downstairs. Can you see what's on the next floor up?'

Joe's only discovery upstairs was a rope that passed through a hole to a large bell above. He smiled at the thought of pulling it… but didn't. There was no way out from there.

Climbing down again, he noticed a collection of metal boxes likely to hold muskets or rifles. Mr Inquisitive moved over to investigate.

Beth returned, out of breath. 'Going down might work,' she said. 'It's all dark, but I think there's a door at the bottom.'

'Look at these,' said Joe.

Beth was not impressed by Joe's find but suddenly caught sight of a two large archery bows resting against the wall. Next to them were two dusty targets with several arrows scattered on the floor nearby. She looked more closely. 'Whoever used this target was a good shot – nearly all bullseyes.' She inspected the other. 'Not like this one. Hopelessly wide of the mark. Look.'

Buzz-ZZZzzz-ZZZzzz-ZZZzzz. A ringing musical noise wobbled through the air as Joe came closer.

'What's that?' said Beth.

'My EAR.'

'Your *ear*? How does that happen? Doesn't it hurt?'

'No, it's my all-energy sensor. Something's triggered it.'

Joe pulled out a small box, the shape of a squashed lemon with bumps, a screen and tiny lights.

'It's telling me we're near a magnetic field.' He moved it close to several objects in turn. 'It's strongest at the targets… but they can't be magnetic. They're only straw and canvas… Unless… inside there's a—'

'Joe! We ought to go!' insisted Beth. 'I know you'd like to find an explanation, but we really have to get to Granelda's cottage. I'm sure she'll make sense of all this. We *will* get caught again if we don't leave soon.'

A sharp sound from the floor above was their final prompt to leave. After they had set off, a large rat scrabbled down from the bell-chamber. If they had stayed, Beth would have noticed a smell of toffee.

As they trod carefully down the stone stairs, the light from above faded. In the tiny space at the bottom, Joe conjured up a soft glow from his PEST.

They had reached a large, round-topped wooden door with a small pane of glass in the middle held by iron. Joe tried hard to push it open, but it was locked. He looked through its metal keyhole but could see nothing.

'Let's try the window?' said Beth. She stood on tiptoes and peered in. 'There's something shining a long way off, otherwise it's all dark.'

'Here, use my PEST on its *Forward Vision* pre-set. You'll get a better view.'

Beth kept her balance while training a bright narrow beam ahead to explore what lay between them and the distant light.

'Official report, Sir,' reported Beth in a military voice. 'A long, blank corridor, about twenty metres.

No windows, no furniture, no pictures. Grandfather clock stationed halfway down. Several – estimate seven – old lamps affixed to the walls: brass and glass – presumed oil-burning. One alight opposite the clock. No personnel visible. And it is completely free of men in shining armour.'

'Thank you, Corporal,' said Joe responding to another of his sister's dramatic turns. 'Forward march!'

'But the door's locked... Sir.'

Joe switched his PEST to 6K:5:25. 'Use this beam. Scan the walls for a hanging key.'

'Yes, Sir!'

Beth began her search... then screamed. Her beam had hit a spider the size of her hand. Its eyes were on stalks and its hairy legs glistened with a milky goo. It was picking its way towards the door from a web high up on the wall, a web that looked more like steel than a flimsy thread.

'Give me the PEST and I'll laser it into vapour!' cried Joe.

'No!' said Beth, holding the PEST behind her back. 'No... don't do that... It's OK. It's... got... a certain smell.'

'A smell! What smell?'

'It's mixture of smells, really. They're good smells.'

'Good smells... from a giant poisonous spider that's getting closer?'

'We're safe, Joe. The spider has come to help.' Beth's expression had lost its terror.

'To help...? A vicious octoped has dropped in to

lend us a hand, or eight, with a smell that only one of us can sense?' He sighed grumpily. 'We're back in the world of the silver bird brain, aren't we?'

'Look! See what's happening...'

They watched the spider anchor itself at the top of the door then spin an aerial line to float down.

'Here's your PEST. *Please* don't damage it.'

Joe, resigned to Beth's weirdness, changed the lighting to get a better view of the beast sliding towards the keyhole. There, it folded up like a circus contortionist and eased itself into the lock. Its guidewire melted and dripped onto the floor. Metallic clicks followed, then the sound of the lock falling open. The door moved ajar, just a little. Without a sound, Beth pushed it open easily.

'Come on, Joe. We'll leave Aranea Humungous to lock up when we're through.'

Joe had nothing to say.

Moving into the corridor, the Ravens were greeted by cold, damp air and the smell of burnt oil from the lamps.

'This must be the servants' secret tunnel,' said Joe, 'just like the magnificent Millicent mentioned.'

They walked on in silence.

Joe was surprised to find the clock working. He studied a piece of paper fixed to its side showing various times of the day with a name next to each one.

'Hey! Granelda's name is on this list.'

'She *is* real, Joe,' said Beth. 'Told you! Let's keep going.'

Closer to the end of the corridor they saw that the distant brightness came from a lamp shining onto worn stone steps. From above, came the clatter of hurrying footsteps and busy voices.

'Up?' said Joe.

'It's the only way. Deep breath in… We're about to be on stage again.'

Reaching the top of the stairs, they knew exactly where they were: in the main thoroughfare of the Servants' Quarters. Women of differing ages, dressed like Beth, were finishing their lunch and streaming out of their dining hall. Strange to think that the Ravens had been there earlier that day. It seemed unlikely that their mother was among them now, unless she had also been whisked back to the eighteenth century as a cook or a town crier.

A tall, thin lady with a prominent nose and gold-rimmed glasses came striding towards them. Her black dress without an apron and the way she behaved gave Beth the uncomfortable idea that this was the housekeeper. She pounced on Beth at once. 'What is this boy doing in the Servants' Quarters? You must know that it is *strictly* forbidden.' She paused to look over her glasses at Beth. 'And I don't recognise *you* as a member of the household either.'

'I'm sorry, Mrs Bugle,' said Beth, remembering her name from their encounter with the butler. 'I am a casual maid. My mother often waits at the tables in the Servants' Hall, but she couldn't get here today. She suggested I came instead to help out.'

'What's your name?'

'Bethana Lucy Raven, Ma'am.'

'I don't recognise *that*, girl.' She softened a little. 'Then again, I don't usually deal with peasant children. And *you*, boy?'

Joe, having had time to think, presented his 'dilemma': 'I'm Joseph Erasure Crow, Ma'am. Very sorry for being here, but I'm lost. I work with an apothecary in Caladrin. I have to deliver a special medicine to an old lady in Boarham. She is *most* unwell.' To strengthen his story, he pulled out a small bottle of brown liquid from his OAK. 'She lives in Quince Cottages, but I don't know how to find them. I've been to Boarham once before, so I was able to find the back entrance to the Hall. I thought I'd come in and ask the way. That's how I bumped into… er… Miss Beth.'

Mrs Bugle lowered her head and narrowed her eyes. 'How did you get past our guard on the door?'

'There wasn't anyone to stop me when I came in,' said Joe using his well-practised innocent look but wondering what he could possibly say next.

'I see,' said Mrs Bugle. 'Ernest is terribly faithful and conscientious. Then again, he is always bending down to polish his shoes at just the wrong moment. Why? Lord Tresquin rules that our household staff should look immaculate at all times, including the shiniest possible foot-ware. He makes snap inspections. Ernest was caught out once. Just once. Since he was allowed back after his "corrective training", he has become obsessed with shoe polish.'

Mrs Bugle looked at Beth's shoes and seemed reluctantly pleased with their shine. 'I still think just striding in here with no introduction was the height of rudeness, and I cannot see why you couldn't have enquired for directions at Mrs Maggutt's stores across the road. Still, you're here now and the quickest way to get rid of you is for *me* to tell you how to find Quince Cottages. It really is very simple. Perhaps even you can remember it? No point in writing it down. I'm sure you can't read.' She examined Joe's face for signs of intelligence, then said she would try anyway, speaking very clearly and slowly.

'Go out of the entrance that you sneaked through – sneaked, I say – and follow the road to the left, round by the church. Take the second turning right. It's called Shepherd's Way – *Shep... herd's... Way*. At the end, turn left. *Quince Cottages* will be right there. Have you got that in your stupid head?'

'Yes, Mrs Bugle. Thank you very much,' said Joe.

'I'll take you to the door.'

That sentence made Beth's heart sink. She was planning that they would get away together, but at least they had learnt where to find Granelda.

'I hope you find the old lady, Master Crow,' said Beth, trying to make a face to him that said, 'Follow Mrs Bugle's plan anyway. I'll catch up with you when I can.'

The housekeeper and Joe set off to find Ernest. How Beth would get out was a different matter. Whether she could get out at all looked doubtful. As she stood trying to conjure up a plan, a loud crashing noise came from the kitchen followed by shouts of a commotion. Mrs Bugle looked round, severely alarmed – something awful must have happened. The deputy head cook appeared at the kitchen door and shouted for her to come immediately. The kitchen staff were in the middle of preparing a fine evening meal for ten visiting noblemen. A large bird had flown through the window and knocked a whole row of copper saucepans from a high shelf onto the elegant dishes they had already set out below with great care.

Mrs Bugle headed to the mess at full speed, shouting over to Beth, 'Take this stupid boy to Ernest and tell him that he can pass out without inspection.' Her face had lost all colour and her voice trembled. 'I must attend to this ghastly state of affairs in the kitchen. It's a *complete* calamity!'

At this, Beth and Joe hurried to the servants' entrance and its guard, a nervous man with rounded shoulders. Beth was received well as she explained the matter and then moved away from his desk. Joe presented himself and remarked on the reputation of Ernest having the shiniest shoes in Boar Hall – in fact, in the whole country – possibly even the whole world. A broad smile broke out across the guard's knobbly face. They compared their shoes in detail. Ernest's were like black mirrors while Joe's were hiding somewhere under a layer of dust and grime. No contest. Ernest's face lit up. He wished Joe, 'God speed!' and watched him leave. Beth was no longer in view.

Striding out into the sunlight, Joe headed left.

'Boo!' said a nearby shadow.

'Ha! Great plan!' said Joe.

Under the cover of the earnest shoegazing, and with Mrs Bugle distracted, Beth had slipped out to hide round the corner until she could join Joe on the road by the church. They followed Mrs Bugle's suggested route along the cobbled road. Crossing over to turn right, they nearly collided with a coach and horses, earning a rude cry from the driver and angry glares from its well-dressed passengers.

Shepherd's Way was short and dusty. Quince Cottages quickly came into view with number three clearly visible. Their hearts were racing again, but for once, not in fear. The mysterious Granelda *in person* was expecting them. DIGITAL was positive: they had found her.

CHAPTER 5

GRANELDA'S CHALLENGE

'What a rotten smell,' said Joe as they opened Granelda's gate. 'Are you expecting any more helpful creatures?'

'No, it's just wild garlic.'

'I guess round here it has to be wild…'

They crept up the neat, flower-edged path, knocked loudly on the door and waited.

No one answered.

He tried harder, but still no response.

'Are you sure we've come to the right place?' said Joe.

Beth checked the gate. 'It's number three – and the sign on the wall said, "Quince Cottages".'

'Maybe we're DIGITAL negative after all. I could

melt the lock with my laser or use my two hundred-decibel dog-whistle to crack open a few windows.'

'No, Joe, we could *not*...' said Beth. 'She could just be out.'

'*Okay*... Why don't we look in the window anyway?'

'Do think we should?'

'A quick peek?'

Joe leapt onto an upturned flowerpot to get a good view over the herbs on the windowsill. 'No sleeping grandmas here,' he reported, 'though she's got a favourite chair by the fireplace.'

As he looked harder, his stomach lurched. This was the last thing he wanted to see. Should he tell his sister? No... Yes... Probably – not that he wanted to.

'Beth... I've just seen a silver bird on the mantelpiece.'

'Oh, really? Like mine?'

'...Yes.'

'Can I see?'

In a single jump, they swapped places. Beth looked towards the fireplace. Seeing the bird's brilliant silver coat and blue eyes, her mind flashed through her sightings of Thyripolis as well as the silver mist and the rainbow scents. She stayed quiet, wondering how much to say, then: 'I'm not sure it's mine, but it must mean we're at Granelda's house. Let's look for a way in at the back.'

They squeezed through a side gate and passed a prickly bush to find a low wooden door. Through its window they saw a simple kitchen. No one was there, and no one came in spite of knocking again and shouting.

'Let's go in anyway, if we can,' said Joe.

'I *think* that would be all right...' said Beth. 'Granelda is expecting us.'

The door opened silently.

Inside, all was quiet and warm. In the centre of the room was a heavy plain table with a few chairs. Pots, pans, cooking tools and ornaments were scattered on open shelves. A large grandfather clock stood near the stairs and a long-bristled brush leant against a wall. Beth noticed a chair with its tall back covered by a shawl facing out of a far window. On the mantelpiece stood a microscope and a model of a three-sailed ship. Above an open fire in a grate hung a large iron pot.

A spicy smell of cooking reminded them that lunch time was ages ago and that they were achingly hungry. Joe saw a plate of cakes on the table, but, remembering the dirty taste of Plaster-of-Paris, he gave them a miss. Beth checked inside the cauldron: brown lumpy soup bubbling gently. It smelled good. Maybe they would be offered some?

A cupboard on the wall made Joe curious. He wandered over to take a look. Getting nearer, his eyes told him that it was shrinking. His head disagreed: *Cupboards don't do that.* His eyes insisted on *their* view and they didn't lie, thank you. Indeed, the closer he got the smaller the cupboard became. He reached up to open it... As soon as he touched its handle, the door flopped down and, to the sound of circus music, four objects jumped down onto a table below. Joe blinked. What were *these?* They were eggs in egg-cups that had legs. When the leg-cups began to jump, their eggs flew into the air and were then caught by another cup in the team. The cups darted around, always throwing their eggs up again, ready to receive the next. In spite of the lightning pace of the game, there were no mid-air collisions and never was a catch missed.

When the music ended in a grand finale, the leg-cups lined up to take a bow. As they straightened up, a smile appeared on each of their eggs. Then they all jumped back into the cupboard and closed the door. Joe and Beth applauded.

With so much noise, the Ravens missed the sound of the window chair moving and the footsteps that followed.

'We call it a *convenience store*, if you didn't know,' announced a sharp, high-pitched voice.

A girl drifted into view, pale and unsmiling. She was a little older than Beth. Her hair was scraggy and her eyes weak. She must have been sitting in the window chair all the time.

'The cupboard knows your thoughts and tries to deliver whatever you are looking for,' she said. '*Of course* it changes size depending on what that is, Joe. You wanted to find something interesting, didn't you? That makes the store bring in all sorts of unexpected objects – though we haven't seen the leg-cups for months. Last time it was a toad reading a poem by William Shakespeare and before that, a flute-playing snake. You have to be careful, though. You can end up with things you *thought* you wanted but turn out to be horrid.'

'We're terribly sorry that we—' started Beth.

'I'm *sure* you are,' broke in the girl. 'We have been waiting for you for ages.' She inspected them as though judging a parade of misfits. 'Very disappointing. I rather thought you would look, well, older and bigger, and *properly* brave. You might have to lose that big coat, Joe. It really does nothing to make you look impressive. Actually, you look quite stupid.'

'But—' began Joe, more bothered about losing his OAK than his coat.

'And as for Little Miss Scullery Maid here, how can *that* be a heroine's costume?'

Beth tried very hard to take no notice. 'You aren't… Gran—' said Beth.

'No…' said the girl. 'I'm not creaky old Granelda, if that's who you mean. She's upstairs. Asleep. I'm Merrin. She's my great aunt. I'll go and tell her you're here… at last. Knowing her, she'll be *very* pleased to see you, though I don't think you're going to be any help. Certainly no help to me.'

For a time Merrin stopped to stare into the distance. Beth and Joe couldn't think of anything useful to say before she turned to walk upstairs. When she did so, her climb was stiff and slow. Her face, if they could have seen it, would have told them she was in pain.

'What was all that about?' said Joe. 'What's wrong with her?'

'I think she had been crying,' said Beth. 'Maybe she's ill?'

'A "hello" would have been nice anyway. We've

nearly been chopped in half and missed lunch to get here.'

'But we'll be meeting Granelda any minute. *She* wants us here anyway.'

'I hope we can get some soup and cake.'

A creaking stair announced Granelda's arrival. When she appeared in the kitchen, her face, though tired, brought an easy, welcoming smile. She looked younger than they expected, but the hair poking out under her white cap was streaked with grey and her shoulders hung heavily.

'Beth… Joe… you have got here! Thank you, and well done! I am so glad that my parcel made its way to you and that you've found help from Thyripolis and the *Guide*.' Granelda smiled at each of them in turn.

Joe looked at the floor.

'I know they trouble you, Joe, and that you don't like not knowing how they work. Maybe in time – perhaps even while you are here – you can come to enjoy what they bring, even if you can't understand them. Anyway, you will do great things to help others, I know. And to you, Beth, let me just say, "Keep going!" You're both on the right track.'

The Ravens felt curiously safe and understood, though they were deeply bewildered.

'I can only guess about your adventures in Boar Hall, but I know that you have already shown yourselves strong and caring enough to take on the task ahead. So… welcome to the past!' She shook her head. 'It's a past where we need all the skills you bring from the future. The menace we are fighting… that we can't solve—'

The grandfather clock whirred and chimed.

'Oh, goodness! It's well beyond lunch time. And I have a meal ready.' Granelda's face relaxed again into a smile. 'For you: spicy beef soup with bread, then boiled rabbit and peas. Joe, I expect you would like a cake or two after that? And Beth, maybe a quince?'

Lit-up faces gave the answer, though Joe tried hard to think of a way to make his peas disappear. The adventurers were served at the table like royalty.

'I am so glad you were able to meet Merrin, though I think you will have found her rather rude?'

Beth and Joe stared into their soup.

Granelda understood. 'Until a few weeks ago she was very different – friendly, cheerful, kind. She used to visit me often. She would run to help me from her home on the other side of the village. Then her parents – such caring souls – began to change. They became irritable and fussy. Their anger flared up at the slightest thing… and they were never like that before. Their arms and legs grew stiff and painful, then so did the rest of them. They lost their hearing and began to go blind. Poor Merrin had to spend night and day looking after them.'

'What happened about her school?' asked Beth.

'School? No one goes to school here. Most children work on the land or help at home…

'One afternoon, she ran to me in tears and terrible distress. After her parents' daily rest, she had peeped into their room. They looked white, a shiny white. When she touched them they were cold and hard. Their faces showed pain and horror. They had no movement, no... life... I'm sure Merrin screamed, but there was nobody to hear her. She ran to find me and we went back to her house together.

'All was just as she had said. If my eyes were true, her parents' clothes were turning white and hard as well. We looked round the bedroom. We looked round the whole house. Everything was normal. And we could think of nothing to help.'

'Couldn't you call a doctor?' Joe asked.

'We have no doctor in the village, Joe. Only the rich in Boar Hall have those. Merrin ran to our apothecary, Mr Chelkwyn. He came at once. Seeing her parents with their faces fixed in pain, he looked puzzled. He tapped their limbs and looked into their eyes. He said he must get them back to his shop to see what he could do. He was trying to sound hopeful but didn't look it. He asked Merrin and me to go back to my house while he made all the arrangements. We were to call on him the next morning.

'Merrin cried and cried. She rushed over to hold her father's hand. It sucked all the heat out of her. Seeing her tears, Mr Chelkwyn remembered his delivery that morning of a new *Golden Silk Elixir* from South America. It was said to be "wonderfully calming in all nervous conditions" and he happened to have a vial in his pocket. Covering his hand with a cloth, he emptied a small amount of the golden liquid into a glass and gave it to her most carefully. Then he left. Merrin and I walked back here with hearts too heavy to speak.'

The kitchen fell silent except for the ticking clock. Beth rested her hand on Granelda's. Joe nursed a headful of questions.

Granelda smiled weakly, gave another deep sigh and continued: 'Next morning, the apothecary's assistant knocked at our door, looking red-faced and terribly troubled. With no explanation, he asked us to come to the shop at once. Mr Chelkwyn was full of dismay and apologies. *Merrin's parents had disappeared overnight.* He had no idea how or where they had gone, and he couldn't think of any way he could find out. When she heard the apothecary's news, Merrin was inconsolable.'

'Did he tell the police?' asked Joe.

'Police? …Yes, I've heard they have those in a few large towns, but in our village, we only have a volunteer night watchman in case of a fire or a street-fight. If there is no moon to see by, they go home. Mr Chelkwyn said he would "tell the local officials directly" – as if that would help. The Duke's officials dance to their master's tune all the time. Their only interest in us is to squash us and take our money.'

'What did Merrin do?' asked Beth.

'She came to stay with me. At first she refused to eat and hardly slept for days. Then something else happened… It was the way she spoke – you have heard it yourself. Her words turned bitter in a way I have never heard before. She began to get stiff muscles and joints. She grew very pale…

'Dear Beth… Joe… she is getting worse by the day and we still haven't found why this has happened. I'm desperately worried that Merrin will become like her parents.'

Joe and Beth thought the same. Neither had much hope for the girl.

'This is the curse, isn't it?' said Beth.

'Yes. It is. A spiteful, *marble* curse that has gripped us without reason. And it has not just fallen on Merrin and her family. Alhicbert – Mr Pinwell – my cousin in Caladrin, has seen people made into statues like her parents displayed on the bridge across the river. The same, shiny-white figures with faces in agony. They appeared overnight last week in spite of a curfew ordered by the Duke.'

'What's the Duke doing to stop it?' asked Joe.

'He has "commanded an inquiry to look into it urgently" – which means, nothing. Nothing will happen. The mind of Lord Tresquin is a pit of darkness… He will protect *himself*, of course, doubling up his personal guard and staying hidden in the Citadel. Meanwhile, new statues are appearing every day. Now they are on show in the city square. I've even heard they have been seen along the drive at Boar Hall.'

Beth and Joe looked at each other.

'You've seen them?' asked Granelda.

They nodded.

'In the age you have just come from?'

'Yes,' said Beth.

Granelda looked down, close to tears. But suddenly,

looking up at the Ravens, her eyes brightened and she sat up straight. 'Then you must change history! When you go back you must find trees along the drive, not people in stone with terrified faces. Can you find out where the curse has come from and how it can be cast out before it destroys us all?'

Joe and Beth looked at each other, then at Granelda.

'We'd *like* to help—' began Beth slowly.

'...and we really can!' said Joe. 'There must be a logical answer and I've got gadgets that will be fantastically useful. We wouldn't have got here without them. We'll get straight on the trail! What you've told us has given me lots of ideas.'

Granelda nodded a smile. 'Thank you. But please stay safe. You mustn't tell anyone where you come from or why you're here. It would be best—'

A sharp knock on the front door stopped the conversation. No one was expected. Granelda looked frightened.

CHAPTER 6

MR GROBE, MR PITH
AND THE COCKROACH

The sharp knock on Granelda's front door came again, louder and more urgently than before.

'I don't know who that is,' said Granelda. 'I had better go – perhaps it's more medicine for Merrin. You two must hide. Joe, jump into the grandfather clock. You'll just fit if you leave your coat in the under-stairs cupboard. Beth, you hide behind the long window curtain. Draw it across a little, then sit on the windowsill so that your feet don't show.'

As soon as Granelda had lifted the door latch, two men with bulging bags pushed their way in. From the waist up, they looked well dressed: three-cornered hats, smart waistcoats and coats. But below, they wore rough trousers – not breeches – and their shoes were covered in dust. They came in full of smiles and, though they had never met her before, they greeted Granelda like one of the family.

'Hello! My name is Atticus Grobe,' said the taller. His voice was friendly, though with sharp edges.

'Hello! My name is Vacuus Pith,' said the other simply.

'We've something to show you,' said Atticus.

'Something *really* special to show you,' said Vacuus.

Granelda tried to turn them away: 'I'm very sorry but I'm looking after a sick girl and it—'

'...must be very difficult for you,' said Atticus. 'I'm so sorry. Is it...' He held a finger to his mouth and whispered, 'The plague? Such a nasty thing, that. But one of the many marvellous samples we've brought is a new carbolic disinfectant!'

'*Brand* new!' said Vacuus. 'And *carbolic*!'

Granelda couldn't stop the salesmen marching towards the kitchen. As they went, Atticus continued: 'It hasn't been tried in cases of plague exactly, but it has been widely used by the nobility.'

'By the *nobility*, including the *King*!' added Vacuus in awe, removing his hat and giving a respectful bow.

They all settled uncomfortably into the kitchen. The clock chimed twice and whirred.

'*Beautiful!*' said Atticus. 'What a distinguished room! And our smart products could make it *so* much more spick and span. And bring much greater hygiene!'

'Hy-giene!' said Vacuus with a warm smile. He

went to shake Granelda's hand, but she quickly pulled it back.

'Now, to business. First, some Impressive Demonstrations,' announced Atticus.

'Please,' said Granelda, 'I really don't want to—'

'Oh, but you *will*, as soon as you see the marvels we can perform in even the most meagre of dwellings.'

'But I am very—'

'Let's start with the filthy windows. Kitchen windows are *always* filthy.' His face looked horrified at the thought. 'Vacuus, you get the glass polish and start with the windows opposite the tall chair over there.'

'No. *No!*' said Granelda. '…If you don't mind. Not *those* windows. I've… got something growing on the windowsill that might die if it's disturbed.'

'Oh. Oh well, these will do. In the back door. You won't have so far to walk, Vacuus.'

Vacuus offered a baby smile and began searching for the polish in one of their bags.

Atticus turned to Granelda. 'I… notice – and, oh dear, smell – that you've been having brown-something soup. Ugh! It's all round the top of the cooking pot. What an awful mess! *But*… we've got *the* magic cleaning solution to dissolve those dribbles away and make it absolutely *shine*! Vacuus, young man, could you throw me over the Soup Cleaner and a Whizz-cloth?'

Vacuus was unpacking a collection bottles and tins, staring hard at the labels on every one. Finally, he chose a clear glass jar that he threw with the Whizz-cloth towards the fireplace. Atticus caught the jar, but the cloth landed inside the cooking pot. Instead, he grabbed one of Granelda's clean towels drying by the fire to spread a large amount of 'magic' liquid where the soup had been spilt.

'Now, Ma'am, just look here! How about *that*!'

An increasingly flustered Granelda moved nearer the action. In an instant, the new cleaning fluid had melted away the soup and was now attacking the rim of the iron pot. It ran down the side, dissolving the metal as it went. With a hissing sound, it gave off an evil smell and black smoke. Soup burst through the long hole and landed on the fire, erupting into clouds of steam and wood ash.

Atticus frowned and looked at the label on the glass jar. 'Vacuus, you *fool*! You've given me the *Super* Cleaner, not the *Soup* Cleaner.'

'*Do* go away now!' pleaded Granelda. 'I've seen quite enough!'

'I am *so* sorry. Of course. I quite understand. You needed that soup for the next meal. Easily put right. Let me just sort it out for you. It will be fine in a minute – then we'll go. You can have our packed lunch to make up for it.'

From behind the curtain Beth was desperate to help, but she dared not move until Granelda gave her the 'all-clear'. Besides, the smoke was beginning to tickle her nose and it took all her concentration not to sneeze.

Atticus coughed his way to the back door and opened it for some fresh air. There he noticed that the windows looked far worse than they did before

Vacuus's attempts to clean them. He picked up the tin of polish. 'Silly, *silly* boy! Why did I bring you at all! I wanted you to use *glass* polish, not *brass* polish. When *are* you going to be able to read?'

He wiped as much of the mess away as possible with Granelda's wet towel.

When the fire finally went out, everything calmed down a little.

'You don't mind if we have a quick drink before we go, do you, Ma'am? Don't worry, there's no need for you to get anything for us. We've got some of our own blueberry and onion squash. It's very good for the digestion.'

'No – of course,' was all an exhausted Granelda could say as she collapsed into a chair and closed her eyes. 'When you've finished, *please… just… go!*'

The salesmen quickly packed away their goods and downed their deep purple drink. Then, suddenly: 'Oh no!' said Vacuus. 'This lovely lady has got a cockroach on her head – and it's crawling towards her face! It must have fallen from a beam in the ceiling in all that smoke.'

Granelda took a sharp breath in, and froze. She was sure she could feel it, even through her cap.

'Quick!' said Atticus. 'Get the spray!'

Vacuus had no trouble in finding the right metal jar with its twisty spray mechanism on top. He shook it, then squeezed hard on its rubber bulb. A misty shower of golden droplets surrounded Granelda's head. She sneezed once, took a deep breath and then, surprisingly, said, 'Thank you! What a lovely smell. Has the cockroach gone?'

'Dead… and…' Atticus moved his hand over her head then into his pocket, '…gone! And *we'll* be gone in an instant too!' he said, smiling broadly.

A shrill voice cut in: 'Get out *now*, you horrible, dirty people. You're just vile tricksters! How dare you push your way into our home and cause an old lady such upset. She could have died of fright! Go! *Go away!*'

Merrin was shouting from the stairs, though how long she had been watching, no one knew.

Atticus and Vacuus moved quickly to leave the kitchen. Glancing back, Vacuus looked Merrin in the eye and said, 'I hope you get better soon, Miss.' As he closed the back door, Atticus added under his breath, 'But you might not. Either of you.'

Granelda, still flopped in her chair, closed her eyes and took a deep breath – then coughed.

Beth jumped down from the windowsill and moved to join the others.

The clock chimed twice, which had a remarkable effect on Granelda. With a dramatic burst of energy, she suddenly jumped out of her chair and ran towards it. 'Oh gracious! *No!* The time has gone so quickly,' she said. 'This means our plan has failed already!'

She grabbed open its doors and looked inside. 'Just as I feared. This is *terrible!*' she said. 'Joe has been whisked away. Why didn't I think of that? Oh… dear! Beth, this is a Post-clock. It's made to take parcels and letters to different places, like the Servants' Quarters in Boar Hall. It's a system we've kept secret for years. Joe has been carried off and I don't know where. I can't think what will happen to him. What a—'

'Stupid!' said Merrin, coming further into the room. 'You can easily find out where the silly boy has gone. Why all the drama? Look at the timetable.'

'Oh… Oh, yes… What a good thought, Merrin,' said Granelda. 'What's the time now?'

'Just after half past three,' said Beth.

Reading a list of figures on the side of the clock, Granelda's face lit up with relief. 'Oh, Beth, it's a delivery to Mr Cringe. He is one of the partners in an extraordinary Manufactory near Caladrin. He is a wonderful old friend and knows of our plan to bring you to us. Joe can introduce himself when he gets there.'

'*When* – or *if*?' said Merrin. 'And how is he going to stop the curse?'

'We don't know that yet!' said Granelda with surprising sharpness. 'That's what Beth and Joe will be helping us find out.'

'Oh, how clever they'll be! Not like us, of course. Anyway, do you think Joe survived the journey in a small box made for parcels? Parcels don't have to breathe.'

Beth and Granelda looked at each other. The colour in their faces drained away.

'How long would the journey last?' asked Beth quietly.

'Who knows – twenty minutes, half an hour?' said Granelda.

'Too long,' said Merrin. 'He'll be delivered dead. I am *so* sorry… Maybe.'

'No! No! That can't happen!' cried Beth with pleading looks at the others. 'It can't!'

'I'm afraid the "new science" has proved it can,' said Merrin. 'Joe would know all about this, wouldn't he? He has heard about the Air Pump experiments, surely?'

'Oh, this is a nightmare!' said Granelda. 'If he *has* died, it will be all my fault. I… am… so… sorry, Beth.'

'Oh *dear*!' said Merrin. 'Your saviour from afar has unexpectedly been, shall we say, "removed from action" by his friends. Not in the plan you had in mind, perhaps?'

'Merrin! Please go upstairs now and take your horrid words with you. We've had enough!' said Granelda.

'Always happy to share my pain,' said Merrin with a pretend smile. 'But I'll make a move if it helps.'

As Merrin turned awkwardly to go, an idea sprang into Granelda's mind. 'Beth, did Joe carry anything, special things that he brought with him?'

'No, he didn't. Everything like that was left behind in his coat pocket.'

Granelda sighed heavily. 'Would he use the *Guide* – if he had it?'

'He should have it. He slipped it back into his breeches' pocket after we'd stunned the dog in Boar Hall. He might think of it… though I don't know if he would look at it even if he was in real trouble.'

'*What* a bright boy!' said Merrin. 'All right, I *am*

going up. I need to. My brain can't cope with idiots.' She started climbing the staircase. A few aching steps later, she paused. 'There wasn't really a cockroach, you know. I saw what happened. It was all pretend – a game to get you to delight in their "miracle" yellow spray. Oh, and do smell the patch of "blueberry and onion squash" that the fools spilt on the floor. It's sicky-fishy not fruity. That's why the awful pair screwed up their faces when they drank it. Wrong label again! Stupid – *squared*!'

Merrin steadied herself by holding on to the wall, took one painful step after another and disappeared from view.

Granelda and Beth sank into chairs, fearful of Joe's life but drained of energy and ideas. In the gloomy silence that followed, the ticking of the clock sounded louder than ever.

Beth glanced up. 'Look! Granelda, look at the clock! There's Thyripolis!'

Perched on the top, the silver bird looked radiant. His warm mix of silver, turquoise and peach looked both muted and vibrant at the same time. He flew down and looked steadily at each them. When their eyes met his, a wave of unexpected calm wrapped around them like a blanket. Words were unnecessary; his stillness gave them hope. No pictures filtered into their minds, nor an understanding of what would happen, but the outcome would be all right even if pain was necessary on the way. Granelda and Beth shared hugs and tears, while the silver bird flew towards the clock, dissolving into mist as he went.

'How can we find out where Joe is?' asked Beth.

'We might get a wiff, otherwise we will have to wait until tomorrow when you can catch a wherry to the wharf.'

Beth could well have used a translation of this but chose simply to trust the words and strength of Thyripolis while she waited for news the next day.

'I haven't spoken much about Thyripolis, have I?' said Granelda. 'There is a lot I need to tell you in time, but a few things might be useful for you to know now. Some people, like Joe, at the moment, can only see him sitting on a shelf like an ornament or a puzzling toy. Others, like you, can see that he really is alive. He can fly. He can understand our thoughts as well our words and "speak" to us silently. I think you've found that for yourself, haven't you?' Beth nodded. 'He knows many things we don't and sometimes things that we can't. And you can never tell where he will pop up.'

Granelda closed her eyes and lost herself in thought.

'Tell me more – please,' said Beth.

'Well, you have seen his extraordinary colours…'

They both looked to the top of the clock to get another view.

'Oh! He's gone again!' said Beth.

Her pang of disappointment was deep, but she began to understand that he would be back again, when he chose, and that this would be all right.

'As I say… you can never tell…' Granelda smiled. 'Anyway, his remarkable colours… he doesn't always wear these. He can stay as a bird and change his appearance or become something quite different – though usually something alive. You might know he is near by a strange, silvery mist or by an invisible scent like nothing you have met before.'

Beth's face beamed. 'He's shown me these already!'

'Has he? That's wonderful. I'm so pleased! One more thing: don't forget you can call on him for help. He may still not appear in the way you have already found him, but in some form, help will come at the right time.'

Beth looked to the top of the clock again and wondered. 'How do you call him?'

'It is very simple: you just have to think of him very hard and talk to him – in your head or out loud – as though he were close by. He usually is, even if out of sight. From the appearance of Thyripolis just now, I think you *will* be meeting Joe tomorrow with Mr Cringe at his famous Manufactory.'

'Let's find you some sensible clothes for your visit and hope that they don't get too dirty in the boat.'

A long-haired dog barked three times outside the front door. Granelda looked troubled again. Was this good news or bad?

CHAPTER 7

WOOLLIE, HADDOCK AND CRINGE

Joe had squeezed into the grandfather clock only moments before Granelda's visitors knocked for the second time. He had expected to bump into hanging weights and a pendulum, but to his surprise, these were missing. Even so, it was a painfully tight fit. The great nonsense of wearing old-fashioned clothes made it even more difficult.

Solid darkness and a sharp smell of timber surrounded him while a loud ticking hammered his head from above. Moving was impossible and he soon felt very hot. His eyes adjusted slowly until he could begin to see his hiding place – a rectangular box outlined by a faint light shining through thin cracks between its wooden planks. Not much air came through those and it was already growing stuffy. The thought gradually infected his mind that if he stayed there too long the box could become his coffin.

'Stop it!' he said, cross with himself for even beginning to panic. Gripping hard on to his logic he argued that by staying completely still he would need less oxygen and all would be fine. One of the cracks was close to his nose, so the carbon dioxide he breathed out could escape well enough. Probably.

An echoing chime made him twitch – not panic, just tension. Granelda had instructed him to hide. Fine. But his body was crying out for air. He must push open the door – push it with all his strength. Nothing moved. Could he bang on the door for help? No. Even if he could be heard, forget it! For whatever reason, his keeping out of the way was important; so he tried to take very slow, very shallow breaths.

His leg hurt. It was hardly surprising in his crunched-up shape and those clothes, but the pain became so intense he had to do something about it. He contorted himself into unnatural angles to reach the spot. It turned out to be a pocket in his breeches. Something solid was sticking into him. Getting it out needed even more twisting and squirming. With his oxygen supply vanishing fast, a growing drowsiness was spreading over him. One... more... *heave* – he had the thing in his hands.

It was oblong and flat. Along three of its thin sides was a fine line of dazzling brightness. His waistcoat reflected enough light for him to see what it was: his useless *Guide*! With a mixture of anger and curiosity, he squeezed his eyes against the glare and flicked it open. Sunshine poured in, and when his vision returned, he saw sky with green fields and trees, all beyond a half-open window.

The window was real. So was the breeze that blew through it. Instantly – automatically – he took a deep breath of fresh air, then another… and another. His head cleared. He cooled down. He could think again – not that he knew *what* to think on this day of constant weirdness. Moving the book around changed the view outside, but the light and air still flowed in. Maybe he could survive for a while longer…

The ticking of the clock continued. His heart thumped heavily at the same speed. What was happening in Granelda's kitchen to take so long? Surely someone must soon let him out.

The clocked chimed again, but this time, something rattled. Joe's prison cell started vibrating. A sharp metallic sound, a wooden creak, then a sudden jolt. His cocoon started to move, and the ticking faded away.

Joe's box gained speed. The lumpy ride that followed threw him painfully around unexpected twists. He sensed he was travelling downwards and along, but how far and how fast, he had no idea. After what felt like a day and a half, Joe's view through his window darkened. Hardly any air blew in and his cell became cold and damp. On the windowsill was a brass oil lamp, though he had not noticed it before. In the middle of the growing darkness its wick suddenly caught fire. The flame, though small, brought comforting illumination and warmth. After passing through a patch of air smelling of rotting fish, he found himself travelling upwards, feet first.

Joe stayed upside down until he thought his head would explode, but the oil lamp disappeared and fresh air burst through his window again. He began to hear the familiar sound of ticking and with a bone-crunching jolt, the box stopped dead. Now what? He guessed he was far away from Beth and Granelda, and he was desperate beyond measure to get out.

He shouted, 'Hello!' with as much air as he could find.

Footsteps. Then a click. His cage doors were pulled open. As they moved apart, two tiny frogs jumped in, bright yellow and very ticklish. They scrabbled past him into a dark corner.

'Oh, pomegranates!' came a voice. 'Why do I always drop things? They're prancing all over the place. Oh! Oh, hello!'

Joe had been spotted. A boy about his age with a long face and nose peered into the clock.

'You're not a parcel!' it said.

'No. I'm Joe, upside down and very squashed.'

'But *someone* must have posted you...'

'Oh... er... an old lady I know,' said Joe, careful not to mention Granelda by name in case it would bring her trouble. 'Can you help me out, please?'

'Sorry. Protocol takes precedence! I must check the timetable first.'

The boy disappeared. More frogs moved towards

the clock but leapt away at speed as Joe started to squeeze himself out.

The boy returned, mumbling, 'Peculiar! Must be the central Boarham Branch.'

'Give me a pull. I'm stuck!' called Joe. '*Please!*'

The boy grabbed his arm and wrenched him out of the clock. Joe stood up slowly on jelly-tingling legs. Surreptitiously, he slipped the *Guide* back into his pocket.

The boys stood looking at each other.

'A perpendicular person! Presented perfectly the right way up. What can I do for you? Did you want to see our catalogue? It's *wonderful!*' said the boy with a permanent look of surprise.

'You could tell me where I am, please – and… what I should call you?'

'You could call me the Lord High Sheriff of Biggleswade if you like, but I usually answer to "Sash". That's short for Sacheverell – Sacheverell Omnin Cringe. At your service!'

'Thanks, Sash. I'm Joe Raven.'

'A pleasure!' said Sash.

Joe had no idea where he had landed. He quickly scanned his surroundings then asked, 'And we are in—'

'…ventive? Yes, we certainly *are* inventive! You *must* stay to see what we do. *We* are Woollie, Haddock and Cringe. Mr Jarek Z Cringe is my father. We have been *appointed* – appointed by His Majesty, King George III. There's no one like us… Pulverising!'

'What do you all do?'

'Everything. Import, design, make, deliver anything and everything needed by apothecaries, philosophers, the new scientists, doctors, and occasionally, alchemists. And lots of other things for the manufactories popping up all over England. Pervasive! Are you sure you don't want to see our catalogue – or look round?'

'No thanks – not yet, anyway,' said Joe, though it was hard to resist an invitation to explore Sash's world.

'Perfect.'

'Sash… I don't know what I'm doing here. It must be a mistake. Sorry. You don't have any ideas, do you?'

'Didn't Granelda tell you?'

'Granelda! Do you know Granelda?'

'Perfunctory! The timetable said you came either from Quince Cottages or Mr Chelkwyn, the local apothecary – they're both on the same clock-line. Since you said "an old lady" sent you, it must have been Granelda. We used to send lots of our goods to her husband until he was taken… to the Well… Putrid punishment!' Sash looked troubled. '…Anyway, Father said we might expect two young friends of Granelda who would come from a long way away to stay with us. You could be one of them, I suppose. If so, you're unexpectedly premature. And we're missing someone else. Perplexing!'

'Yes, that's it – that's me! The other person is my sister, Beth.'

'Pretty? Is she coming by clock?'

'I don't know. Probably not – she wouldn't fit in.'

'By balloon, perhaps? Dr McFudgett has got this paralysing new invention. Have you seen it? We've spotted it in the air sometimes. Petrifying! Or possibly a boat up the river?'

Something brightly coloured flashed in and out of Sash's view. 'Pestilential perambulators! The frogs! They're due to be delivered before tomorrow. Help me catch them!'

'Shall I get the two that jumped in the clock?'

'Yes – but watch out. It's due to leave again in five minutes. You'll need two hands to scoop them up. We've sixteen to find. Put them in here.'

Sash carefully placed a large, globular glass jar on a chair nearby and the boys set off at speed on Operation Capture. Joe snared the first frog almost at once, but opening the jar's heavy metal lid without losing the frog was fiddly. Eventually, fifteen frogs were caught, the last one still hiding inside the clock no matter what.

'Polished performance!' said Sash. 'Don't worry about the sixteenth; it will proceed *pari passu* to the proper place.' He moved the jar of frogs with their water and airspace into the clock, then closed its doors. 'Pleasing!' he said, shaking Joe's hand. 'Thank you again. Another batch of Golden Frogs perfectly on its way. We import them from Panama, you know.'

'Where's that?' asked Joe.

'Down… and then sideways… probably left, I think. Why don't we perambulate round the Manufactory and I'll introduce you to Father? He's chemistry. Mr Haddock is living things, and Mr Woollie makes machines – particularly promising in mechanics and optics.'

Joe needed no second invitation.

They quickly reached a wide wooden door with hinges on one side and a sturdy black handle on the other.

'Try the handle,' invited Sash.

Joe pressed it down, but with no effect. He tried again with greater pressure, but it still didn't move. He wondered if doors ever opened easily in this crazy place.

'Ha-ha! Purposeful! The door doesn't open that way! You see, to keep out *bad people* it's a pretend lock. We've fixed a sneaky one that really does work. It's digital, look… in the doorpost.'

Joe found a small box with four holes in a row.

'You put a finger in each hole to activate the levers that move the opening mechanism. But you must press them in the right order to get in. If you get it wrong – even once – you get sprayed with red itchy paint. In practice, pretty well perfect!'

Sash demonstrated how it worked. Within seconds, the middle section of the door sank into the ground completely. He jumped swiftly into the long corridor beyond while Joe stopped to explore the workings of the door.

'Peanuts! Propulsion needed. Press on! The door pushes up again automatically in the shake of peacock's tail. It's all done by pressure and pistons. Come on!'

They wandered into the depths of an enormous stone building. Corridors with high windows ran in all directions. Noises, smells or smoke filtered out underneath all the doors that Joe could see. Workmen were moving trolleys everywhere, piled high with instruments, strange-coloured jars, animals (alive or dead), powders, plants, tubes, glass, boxes, fish tanks, clocks, planks of wood, magnets… In the distance men were pushing barrow-loads of coal towards the Watt & Boulton steam engines that powered the Manufactory's many machines.

'Brass and glass, petals and metals, hawks and corks – we've got it all here in plenty,' said Sash. 'Let's see if Father is in.'

They squeezed their way past a trolley carrying a curious-looking gadget with four large brass tubes and lots of smaller ones with taps and connections.

'That's a Quadruple-Barreled Air Pump. The biggest one out. It's used for demonstrating that rats die if they don't get enough air,' said Sash.

'I know how they feel,' said Joe quietly.

'Oh! And here's a cart laden with Leyden jars. You're from the Parishes, aren't you, so I'm positive you've not seen one of those. They store electricity that works like *lightning*! Profound! And powerful! We send some of these to Dr McFudgett.'

Joe made a sound that meant 'gosh, that sounds interesting' but said nothing that would give himself away. A screeching whistle broke into the conversation – his EAR again! How could that happen? He fumbled in his pocket for the mute button but was unable to reach it before Sash, hands over his ears, shrieked, 'Ouch! What's *that*?'

'Tinnitus?' said Joe, pretending that nothing was wrong. 'Ringing in the ears. Sorry you've got that. It sometimes happens when you are close to very high charges. My mother told me that recently at a check-out. Let's move away from the jars.'

Calm was restored, but not for long. When a trolley with magnets and lodestones went past, Joe's EAR sprang into action again, producing the same *buzz-ZZZZ-zzzz* that was triggered by the archery targets in the round tower. Fortunately, Sash thought this to be one of the Manufactory machines going wrong.

Passing the Optics wing, Sash picked up a magnifying glass the size of his head. 'Let me see what you are made of,' he said, holding it a few inches from Joe's nose. 'Peppered freckles, putrid spots, pea-green eyes, but no protuberant nose hairs. Passable!'

'I can see you too,' said Joe. 'Your face looks like the surface of the moon.'

Sash pulled a screwed-up expression and stuck his tongue out.

'…and… your eyes are not the same colour,' Joe continued. 'Woops! Should I have said that?'

'Perspicacious! And a permissible proclamation,' said Sash. 'The blue one is the original. I am told the other one went brown when a tiny speck of *remonscrentium* flew into it. My father was carrying me round the Manufactory as a baby at the time.'

'Oh, I'm so sorry,' said Joe. *Remonscrentium? What's that?*

'No need. It's peculiar, but purely personal and perfectly passive. It means I can blink in two colours.

Though I suppose it might be difficult to find a matching wife.'

They moved on.

'Here's Father's laboratory,' said Sash, stopping by a door. A shiny green vapour was pouring out of the keyhole. 'Portentous, but penetrating! I think this might be *gold confabulate*. He's been trying to make some for a long time.'

Sash took a closer sniff, then shook his head. 'No. Pity. Probably, it's aromatic toenails; they make a good glue if ever you run short.'

He knocked at the door. A squeaky voice replied, 'Mr Cringe is out. Please call later.'

'That's Peregrine, the office parrot... Pigs! That means Father is away until tomorrow, sorry. Well... let's have a peek in Mr Haddock's patch.'

They walked to a more open area past stacked cages, fish tanks and kennels, all containing a most remarkable collection of living things. A large pond offered a breeding ground and a temporary residence to the Golden Frogs, as well as to something that looked like part of a deep-sea monster. Just outside was the Garden of Herbs & Poisons. *What was rhubarb doing there? No wonder school lunches were deadly.*

Mr Haddock was 'IN'. His beard was home to half of his insect collection, and when Joe and Sash met him, his face was covered in woodlice. He could open his eyes a little and seemed pleased to see the boys. He would have smiled generously had it been safe to do so.

'Just trying out a new roodlice rehellent,' he voiced

deeply, unable to move his lips. 'It should regin to rork soon. You could rait, or you can have a riff if you like.'

'I propose the wiffs,' said Sash.

'Really?' said Joe.

'Yes! Passionately! You'll love them – they are very talented and hardworking, and cuddly, in a way. Proceed!' Sash brought a dazed Joe to a row of cages, each holding two beefy, long-haired animals of different colours. 'They're Portuguese Water dogs.'

Joe looked blank.

'They're another part of our s-s-secret network, like the Post-clocks,' said Sash. 'Their long hair never stops growing. You can harvest chunks of it for making pouches to carry messages or short letters. When you tie the pouches back on the dog, they look just like its original coat… and *nobody* notices. The dogs don't mind either; they look great. In fact, they admire themselves in a mirror when the pouches have been placed.'

Joe was getting more and more convinced that he had slipped into a world going mad. Or maybe it was all a dream. *If so, please could I wake up?*

'Sash, that's all really interesting, but can we get back to your place, please – or wherever I can stay tonight for a rest. I haven't been, like, lying in the sun all day, and I'm worried about Beth and Granelda. They must think I have got lost, or worse.'

'Polite! How very polite! And kind!' responded Sash. 'Of course. I'll just say that the dogs are called "wiffs" because that's how they find where to make their delivery. We teach each of them a catchy smell at WH and C – like rose, or garlic, or liquorice – then they hunt for the same smell to find the house where we want them to go. Planning is precise. Each member of the Archers has a particular smell by their gate or front door, then on arrival, the wiff barks three times to gain entry. Nobody is interested in a stray dog wandering around.' He looked quickly from side to side. 'And no one from the Citadel has yet spotted our s-s-secret delivery system at work.'

Joe's central processor was overloaded: Post-clocks? Yellow frogs? Wiffs? An idea clicked into his mind: 'Is Granelda on your list of contacts?'

'Present and correct.'

'Then we could send her a note now using one of your wiffs?'

'Possible? Absolutely. A pleasure. Distance no problem. Too late for a post-note anyway. She's Tincture of Iodine, if I remember rightly – or is it Garlic?'

'Garlic,' said Joe, recalling the awful smell that greeted them when they arrived at Quince Cottages.

And so it was done. After training it in the right smell, a wiff called Colin was dispatched with a short note from Joe announcing his safe arrival at Woollie, Haddock and Cringe.

There was so much more to see, but a meal and a bed in Sash's house was all Joe longed for. He had escaped being torn apart by a hound, being chopped in half by an armoured knight and dying of oxygen starvation – enough for one day. Tomorrow? Tomorrow might be easier...

CHAPTER 8

THE PLANNING ROOM

The next day in Granelda's house started with toast, homemade quince jam and an egg.

'Eat *quickly*, Beth!' said Granelda. 'I must walk you down to the river to catch our wherry. Don't forget Joe's coat – and mind your dress! It's Merrin's and she'll be angry if you get it dirty.'

They walked through the twisty streets of Boarham to join a path from Boar Hall to a small riverside jetty. Granelda was cross with the stones that made her stumble and complained at the smell of a bridge they had to pass under. She was even more annoyed when they arrived at the jetty to find no one there.

'Why are our plans not working at all?' said

Granelda. 'I sent a wiff to remind the boatman only this morning!'

'I'm sure he'll be here soon,' said Beth. She could see a small boat moving towards them from between the ships in the harbour.

The boatman apologised for his delay – his oars had become tangled in some rigging. Granelda scowled but said nothing. He helped Beth into the boat as Granelda shouted, '*Do* mind that dress, and try to get things *right*. We have only one chance to overcome the curse!' Her face was sullen and as the boat moved away from the jetty, she offered neither a 'Goodbye!' nor a wave.

The boatman rowed easily upriver towards Caladrin. He told Beth about the grand ships bringing extraordinary things from across the world. He also splashed water over Beth's borrowed clothing. On the far side of the river ran a towpath where powerful horses were pulling barges of people and goods from the harbour to the city.

'The river's too shallow for galleons,' he explained. 'Everything has to move on smaller craft to reach Caladrin.'

As the boat navigated a bend, the walled city came into view, clinging to a steep hillside. Houses with red roofs crowded towards the bottom while a single winding track snaked upward from the back of the town to the Duke's Citadel high at the top. The boatman pointed out a bridge with towers at each end that crossed the river from the city entrance to a road on the other side. Staring at the bridge, Beth saw a long line of mottled-white figures. They looked as crushed as those she remembered from Boar Hall the day before, when she was still in the twenty-first century.

The boatman stopped rowing. 'You know about these?'

'Yes. People think it's a curse, don't they, though no one knows where it comes from?'

'I dunno about curses, but it's evil. If it was an illness, people'd be proper buried. But they're stuck up there for all to see. *Why?* That's what I wanta know.'

'Who do you think is doing it?'

'...Dunno.'

'No ideas?'

'...Can't say out loud. Dunno who you are to tell, do I?'

'But I've come to help.'

'Help? *You?* Against *'im?*' He looked up towards the Citadel then back to Beth. 'Naa. Keep tucked away with Granelda or you'll be on that bridge too.'

'But I'm going to see Mr Cringe to see what my brother and I can do.'

'Really? ...As may be. My advice? Don't get caught up in it.' He looked Beth in the eye. 'But you will, won't you? Got that look about you.'

He started rowing again. 'That's the landing stage, in front of the Manufactory.' The boatman pointed to buildings just outside the city wall. 'That's Woollie, 'addock and Cringe. Remarkable place.'

They moored the boat and the boatman helped Beth out. 'Stay safe,' he said in a kindly way. 'Oh, and we 'aven't spoken at all 'cept about the river traffic – right?'

'Right!'

Coming towards the landing stage was a small figure. 'Hello, Beth!' it shouted as they arrived. Joe had been given the task of bringing her to meet Mr Cringe.

'Spilt breakfast down your dress?' said Joe.

'Say nothing,' said Beth. 'Blame the boatman. It's really good to see you. Are you all right?'

Joe nodded with a smile, then froze while he suffered a sisterly hug.

'Here's your coat.'

'Thanks.' He went straight for his OAK.

'Thanks for your note last evening.'

'Did you think I'd got lost?'

'We saw where you were travelling from the timetable on the Post-clock. Granelda was *so* upset. Merrin couldn't see how you could survive the journey in a closed box underground and across the river. She was expecting you to arrive at the Manufactory, dead.'

'That must have cheered her up!'

'How *did* you get air, Joe?'

'A window opened in my wooden carriage.'

'A window? In a travelling postbox? Why would anyone need that?'

Joe felt cornered into telling Beth what had happened, though part of him was relieved. Anyway, as a scientist, he should report his observations accurately, even if they seemed mad. And he couldn't deny that his sort-of-stupid *Guide* had saved his life. So he described the window, and the wind, and the sunshine, and the oil lamp – and the yellow frogs.

Beth was delighted. Not only had Joe survived, but maybe he had begun to see his *Guide* in a different way. 'Not *too* boring, then…' was all she said.

'I've met a new friend called Sash. He's a bit odd, but his dad is the boss here. And this place is bulging with all the old science you can imagine.'

'Granelda was really cross this morning,' said Beth as they walked to the Manufactory.'That must be unusual. I hope she's all right. By the way, she said that children have to call grown-ups "Sir" or "Ma'am", except their parents.'

'Of course – Ma'am.'

Sash was standing at the large doorway of the Manufactory.

'Welcome to Woollie, Haddock and Cringe,' he said grandly, 'purveyors of perfect products for everyone from petite persons to prolific populations.' Wide-eyed at the new visitor, he added, 'Pretty! Perfectly pretty!' He gave a theatrical bow to Beth and a long wink to Joe, then his face fell. 'Perplexing position, I fear – a preposterous perturbation of our plans. Father is still away. He had wanted particularly to meet you in person. Profound apologies!'

'That's OK. Can we talk to you instead?' asked Joe. 'There's lots of things we want to ask.'

'We'd love to hear what you think about the marble curse. Our home is far away and we don't get much news,' said Beth. 'You must know lots about it.'

Sash turned very slightly red.'A perfect pleasure,' he

said. 'Father gave me permission to talk to you in the *Planning Room*. It's where we pool our perceptions to prioritise our potentially profitable pursuits.'

They moved to a small tidy room with a large table. Bookcases and technical drawings lined the walls except where there was large map. This showed Caladrin and Boarham with the area around. A grandfather clock stood in the corner.

'I'll get you a drink,' said Sash. 'Pineapple pressé, perhaps?'

The Ravens wondered what that was but nodded anyway. While Sash headed for the kitchen, Joe and Beth studied the map.

'There's the harbour where my wherry came from,' said Beth, 'and Boar Hall. And the bridge where the—'

'Look!' said Joe. 'Crosses and names... where the statues must be. Mr Cringe is mapping the victims of the curse.'

'Do you really think it *is* a curse?' asked Beth.

'No, not really. It's got to be something more solid than spooky mumbling from a weird witch. I'm thinking strange chemistry. Have you seen the crosses in the towns?'

There were about thirty of these, guessed Beth – a small collection in Caladrin's town centre and some near Boar Hall.

Sash returned with three glasses of a striped yellow and green liquid. Joe was tempted to analyse it with his Omniscope but kept it in his pocket. It would be difficult to explain.

'Prepared for questions!' announced Sash. 'Propel them my way.'

'We've been looking at the map,' said Joe. 'We think the crosses show where the victims of the curse have been put on show?'

'Precisely,' said Sash. His cheery voice had vanished.

'I'm sorry,' said Beth. 'You know who they are?'

'Pretty well all. Many were family friends.'

'Is there any link between them? Have they got anything in common?' asked Joe.

'Father and Mr Alhicbert Pinwell think they are all supporters of Lord Castus.'

'Mr Pinwell, Granelda's cousin?' asked Beth.

'Yes. He presides over a popular and prestigious bakery in Caladrin. He provides polished pastries for the Citadel by special commission.'

'Alhicbert's an odd name,' said Joe.

'It was meant to be Albert,' said Sash. 'Peradventure, when his father gave his son's name to the Citadel Records, he had hiccoughs. One of them found its way into the middle of Albert.'

'Who is Lord Castus?' asked Beth, then, 'Oh! I know.' She had suddenly remembered the picture that Thyripolis showed her in Boar Hall. 'Didn't Lord Castus play an archery match against his twin to decide who would become the next Duke?'

'Precisely – again,' said Sash, impressed.

'And though Castus was brilliant at archery, Lord Tresquin won.'

Joe looked grumpy. How did Beth know that?

'It was particularly peculiar,' said Sash. 'The archery skills of the poisonous Lord Tresquin were perceived by all to be paltry, yet he scored three straight bullseyes. The arrows of the princely Lord Castus, the people's perfect preference, only peppered the periphery.'

Beth's mind skipped straight back to the portrait she saw in Boar Hall, the pleased-with-himself Duke in front of his winning strikes. Joe's mind jumped to the round tower and the targets that triggered his Energy Alert Responder.

'I know how he did it, how Lord Tresquin won!' Joe announced. '*Magnetism!*'

'Lodestone?' asked Sash. 'How did that perform, precisely?'

Joe explained, 'The contestants were given separate targets. My EAR detected a magnetic field at the centre of one target and all around the edge of the other. The magnetism pulled the arrows towards either the bullseye for Lord Tresquin or the edge for Lord Castus.'

'Philosophising petunias!' said Sash. 'You can *hear* magnetism? Where did you get all that from?'

'6HR science lessons,' said Joe. 'Mr Rampage.'

'Well done, Joe,' said Beth.

'What person could have placed the magnets?' asked Sash.

'The archery supervisor, or whatever he's called,' Joe suggested. 'Easy to push tapered magnets or lodestone into the straw while setting up.'

'Perspicacious. A plausible possibility... Father told me once of a rumour that after the contest, the field steward was found dead in a nearby barn. Had fallen and hit his head.'

'How convenient,' said Joe. 'Lord Tresquin and friends covered their tracks well.'

'So it was all rigged by the selfish beast who is still in control,' said Beth. '...So what now, fine gentlemen? Great work, Joe, but we're not much closer to solving the curse.'

'More pressé, perhaps?' suggested Sash.

'Just the green if you—' began Joe.

The clock chimed, clattered and flicked a small red flag from its side.

'A post-note!' said Sash, jumping up to investigate.'

He retrieved a warm bun with the letters 'AP' written in currents on top. Joe spotted a small note that had fallen on the floor. 'Come and see what's cooking,' it said, 'and bring the key.'

'A personal invitation from Mr Alhicbert Pinwell,' pronounced Sash.

'Yes! He'll know more,' said Beth. 'Where's the key?'

Joe, with his detailed knowledge of clock travel, explored the transport carriage. There it was, a key wedged in a crack between the wooden boards. He showed it to Sash.

'Perceptive! It's a padlock key to pass through the city wall between the Manufactory and a road to the Square. A privilege to take you there – if you please – though I'll have to push back pronto. I must process a batch of *remonscrentium* before it particulates.'

The chime of one-thirty launched the afternoon's expedition. With keys, coats and the OAK, all three walked towards the city centre hoping that Mr Pinwell could cook up something useful for their mission.

CHAPTER 9

UPHILL

Mr Pinwell's Bakery stood out on a corner of the main square. The shoppers crammed inside were rapidly scooping up cakes and truffles. They didn't notice a long-haired dog with tell-tale icing on its nose squeezing between their legs. It also had a suspicious patch on its body. *I wonder how many people know that's a wiff*, thought Joe.

Sash led the way through the crowd. 'Pardon... A parting through, please... Pardon us.'

Joe and Beth followed him to the back of the counter.

'Hello, Mrs Pinwell, Ma'am,' he said. 'I'm just propelling Joe and Beth to see Mr Pinwell, if permitted. He has precipitated a prior, personal appointment.'

'Good. And welcome!' said Mrs Pinwell, looking at Beth and Joe with cheerful curiosity. 'Free samples, children?'

Three pastry cones were handed over, each filled with cream and strawberry jam, a little of which fell out, unnoticed, onto Beth's dress. Mrs Pinwell led them towards the kitchen and pushed open the door. The three cream-smeared noses were immediately overtaken by a glorious smell of baking – and the fierce heat from a stone oven. Its fire was in full view. Mr Pinwell was wielding a long-handled shovel to remove freshly baked rolls – tangy cinnamon, this batch. He was a muscular, red-faced man with a big nose and a no-nonsense expression. He nodded at his visitors: 'Meet in the Cosy.' Sash led the way but waited outside until Mr Pinwell pushed past and opened the door.

His back room was indeed cosy – small and stuffy. On the walls hung any number of certificates of Outstanding Achievement in Baking as well as a crested Appointment to the Duke of Curdlingshire. The floor and the furniture, as well as most of Mr Pinwell, were covered in flour.

'Thank you for seeing us, Sir,' said Sash. 'This is Beth and Joe.'

Mr Pinwell nodded again but said nothing.

'My pardon, but I must return promptly to my preparations. Father sends his profound greetings. Thank you again, and goodbye!'

Sash bowed and left, narrowly missing Mrs Pinwell carrying a tray of chocolate spirals.

'Brass tacks, then,' said Mr Pinwell. 'Cousin Granelda wants me to help you. No idea where you're from. "Somewhere special," she says… Hmm. No matter. Sweet lady. Happy to do anything for her. About the curse, isn't it?'

'Yes, Sir,' said Joe.

'Don't bother with the "Sir", boy. "Mr Pinwell" will do. You're family, for now. Coat off. Get comfortable.'

His visitors squashed themselves into a single armchair. When the cloud of flour had settled, he continued: 'Right! What do *you* think about the curse?'

'It's a curse for a reason,' said Joe.

'It's horrid!' said Beth. 'It's poisonous – *so*… mean.'

'Course it is. That's what curses are – so they say. I don't hold with them at all. Curses? Ghosts? Goblins? Never. Beth, you said "poisonous". Right! Quite right! We're not being cursed – we're being poisoned!'

Mr Pinwell leant forward and spoke softly: 'Not said that to Cousin Granelda. Might be upset.'

'What's the poison, Mr Pinwell?' asked Joe.

'No idea. Just seen what it does.'

They were all silent for a moment, picturing the disfigured statues on the bridge.

'We don't know who's doing this, do we?' said Beth.

Mr Pinwell shook his head.

'Sash said you thought it might be to do with the supporters of Lord Tresquin,' said Joe.

'An idea,' said Mr Pinwell. 'Might be right. Might not. So far, it's standing up.'

'Can you tell us more, please?' said Joe.

'Hmm. You know about the crooked contest of 1774?' began Mr Pinwell.

The Ravens nodded.

'When it was over, the twins made speeches. Tresquin was odious, full of himself. False humility. Big empty promises.' Mr Pinwell paused and his face darkened. '*Vermin!*

'Castus spoke next: gracious. Genuine. Warm-hearted. Said he couldn't stay – leaving by boat within the week. Promise he'd come back. Some sort of poetry about Mars and Jupiter. Often spoke in riddles. Left a few nights later.'

'What about his family?' asked Beth.

'Didn't have one. Too busy. Archery and astronomy.

'Though he'd left the country, the supporters of Castus made a great fuss. Told everyone Tresquin had rigged the match. Made protests. Got arrested – put in prison. Leaders executed for treason or put in the Well. Rebellion didn't last long. Crushed to pieces.'

'What does "put in the well" mean, please?' asked Joe.

'Just that. An old well behind the Citadel. Two hundred feet deep, they say. Could be wet. Could be dry. If Tresquin doesn't like you, his soldiers throw you in. Quick, cheap, tidy. A slow death and burial all in one go.

'Anyway... a few of Castus's supporters, like Mr Cringe, were canny. Kept their heads down – and on. Built this secret society in Caladrin. Called themselves "the Archers". Started in Boarham later.'

'What could the Archers do?' said Beth.

'Nothing much. Have midnight meetings in the Manufactory. Cheer each other up. Listen out for ways to topple Tresquin. Keep quiet.'

'Did anything happen?' asked Joe.

'No. Kept bright for a while. Kept hoping—'

'What for?' asked Beth.

'The return of Lord Castus... Hmph. Never happened. Archers lost heart after a few years. Some still meet.'

'Why?' asked Joe.

'"Keep his spirit alive", whatever that means. They hide. Think spies from the Citadel are always looking for traitors.'

'Are they?'

Mr Pinwell nodded. 'Anyone caught challenging him doesn't breathe for long. Archers top of the list.'

'The statues on the bridge...' began Beth, 'I saw them from the river. I'm *so* sorry about your friends. Were they Archers?'

'Yes. Once.'

'What about the others?'

'Knew a few more of them. Not well. May have included new recruits. Tresquin was always hated.'

'We saw a lot more statues like that on the drive up to Boar Hall,' said Joe.

'How did you do *that*?' said Mr Pinwell, amazed. 'Have to be invited by a King's Noble to ride on the drive!'

'We didn't actually *see* them,' said quick-thinking Beth. 'One of Granelda's friends is a Boar Hall gardener who had seen them. She told us about it.'

Mr Pinwell looked thoughtful. 'Granelda said nothing about that.'

Beth looked at Joe. Joe looked elsewhere.

'Anyway,' said Mr Pinwell, 'Cringe and McFudgett have checked. Every statue they've seen has been an Archer – or a member of an Archer's family.'

Mrs Pinwell flowed in with a tray of drinks and three treacle tarts. 'Have you made any progress with all your talk?'

'Told them it's a poison, not a "curse". Told them it's to silence the Archers. And no one knows who or how,' said Mr Pinwell.

'Well, I've always said it's obvious – Lord Tresquin, surely?' said his wife. 'He's been furious with them since the contest. He's on his guard – frightened, I'd say – in case his twin returns with a battle in mind. He doesn't want the supporters of Castus building up strength.'

'No proof. But you may be right, Mrs Pinwell,' said her husband.

Mrs Pinwell had no doubt she was. 'Well, get some! We can't go on like this,' she said.

'I've got some apparatus that we could use to listen to Lord Tresquin's conversations without being seen,' said Joe. *Have I said too much again?*

Beth frowned.

Mrs Pinwell dismissed the idea: 'I don't know anything about that. Sounds far too complicated and dangerous. Gossip, that's what you need. Simple gossip. The chatter of ordinary people.'

'How do these children do that, precisely, Mrs Pinwell?' said Mr Pinwell.

'Well…' she began. 'As it happens, I've just had an urgent message from the Citadel. Men at an important meeting are short of refreshments. The royal kitchen can't cope and anyway, they want some of our speciality cakes. Now. The crinkly ginger-worm fingers in marshmallow and the beetle-juice meringues with mock cobwebs, Mr Pinwell, please?'

The baker sighed and looked at the ceiling.

His wife continued: 'Beth, why don't you become one of our shop assistants, then you can take a box-full to the meeting. They won't know you. All you have to do is deliver them. While you're there, you can "get lost". You can snoop about and talk to people while asking the way out. Listen to the servants or the low-ranking soldiers. They'll like you and they always know what's going on.'

'She'll get caught, Mrs Pinwell. Too dangerous,' said her husband.

'I'll do it if you think it would help,' said Beth. 'I'm used to changing costumes and playing a part. I'm good at balancing things, too. And I can get lost without trying.'

'Too dangerous, I say,' repeated Mr Pinwell.

'I could go as well,' said Joe.

'Joe, that's thoughtful, but it wouldn't look right,' said Mrs Pinwell.

'Someone's got to deliver the cakes urgently,' said Beth, 'so it might as well be me. I'd enjoy the walk up to the Citadel. There'll be great views from up there.'

'Must check the oven,' said Mr Pinwell. 'Not going to change your minds, am I?' Puffs of flour surrounded him as he went back to the kitchen.

With her next costume change Beth looked every part a regular shop assistant from Mr Pinwell's Bakery. Mrs Pinwell assembled the box of cakes, told her how to find the right way into the Citadel and, with Joe, walked with her to a gate in the wall at the back of the city.

'One more thing,' said Mrs Pinwell. 'You see those arches across the winding path? They are sentry points. Lord Tresquin is very careful about health and safety – his own, anyway. You will need to show today's password at each one and get it stamped. Here it is. I've written it down. Put it in your pocket for safety.'

Joe and Beth walked to the start of the long track up to the Citadel.

'Let me give you a hug before you go,' said Joe with a fleeting nod. Beth was startled at this unusual show of affection until she heard him whisper, 'Take this; it's my RAT.'

'A *rat*!' cried Beth, stifling a scream.

'A Remote Audio Transmitter for listening at keyholes. OK?'

He slid something jangly into her apron pocket. 'Find a key that fits, then click the button on the keyring. Put the receiver in your ear. Nothing else to do but listen – as far away as you like.' He moved back to say out loud, 'Good luck! Don't get too lost. I'll wait for you in the Square.' As she set off he shouted, 'Save me a cake if you can!'

Beth's upward path started gently but quickly became steeper. At the first sentry point, balancing the cake box and the paper for stamping was a challenge. The two guards did nothing to help. They teased her for not learning how to juggle before she became a pastry-maid.

'Give us a marshmallow, lovely girl,' said one in a mock-pleading voice.

'Then we'll stamp your pass,' said the other.

'These are cakes for a very important meeting with Lord Tresquin,' said Beth, trying to sound bigger than she felt.

'Oh, Lord Tresquin – the *Duke*… That *does* sound important, doesn't it, Percy?' said the first.

'Can't upset *him*, can we, Frederick?' said the second.

'They've got beetle-juice inside.' Beth tried to put them off.

'You know, Percy, I've never felt that my constitution was *particularly* happy with beetle-juice,' said Frederick. 'How about yours?'

'Makes my freckles itch.'

'Hm. Better not eat any, then.'

'So… all cakes to be left for the great Lord above us?'

'Better stamp the form, then?'

'Better stamp the form.'

Beth felt their laughter all the way to the next sentry point. How would she be treated there?

The answer was: not at all. The one guard left was deeply asleep. After a moment's hesitation she stamped the form herself.

The next sentry post was empty: no soldiers, no stamp, no notice. That could be a problem. Keep going anyway.

The fourth section of the path was even steeper, only a footstep away from a sharp drop down to the valley. She gripped her box hard against an increasing wind and kept as close as possible to the hillside. At the next post, the guards were tucked inside their shelter, trying to keep warm. As Beth approached, they waved her to come in. The form was ready in her hand, but as she offered it for stamping it was caught by a wild gust of wind. *No!* The paper shot into the air, twisting and diving, finally disappearing behind the trees. She rushed to follow it, but tripped. The cake box tumbled towards the edge of the path. Stretched out on the ground, she grasped it back, but not before it had edged further over the hillside. She sighed, brushed herself down, then straightened the box as much as she could. She wasn't brave enough to look inside.

After a few, slow steps back towards the sentry post, she stopped – and cried. Never mind the soldiers. Never mind the ginger marshmallows. Never mind the 'curse'. She was exhausted – and trapped. Suddenly she couldn't care what happened next, if only she could get back to her real life: friendly archery matches, fun plays, books to read curled up in bed where adventures and fairy-tale birds were confined strictly to their pages. Even mother's endless silly talking would be wonderful. Joe could manage here with all his ideas and gadgets. He might even take more notice of his *Guide* to keep himself out of trouble. How *could* home be two hundred years away?

As she set off again, a fluttering sound tangled with the storm in her head. Through bleary eyes she saw that a black bird had blown inside the sentry post. Its beak was yellow – or was it? A funny shape, anyway. One of the guards moved forwards and stretched out his arm. The bird stayed still, looking at him. Beth screwed up her eyes and looked again at its beak. It *was* yellow, but it had a white piece of paper in it. The soldier took her pass from the bird, stamped it and gave it back. Overwhelmed with relief, she could say only a quiet, 'Thank you.'

'Better get going,' said the guard in an ordinary sort of way. 'Looks like your friend wants to go too.'

As Beth left the sentry post, the bird held on to the cake box. A shimmer of bright silver shot across its feathers.

'I knew it was you,' she said, 'but why are you so black?'

Thyripolis looked at her intently as she plodded up the last section of the path.

'A disguise? No, it's more than that, isn't it?'

Thyripolis lowered his head, looked down and stayed perfectly still. Then his feathers flooded with rich colours interwoven with gold. For a moment he looked like royalty, but he quickly shrank back into his deep black coat. Beth looked hard into his eyes. They were dull in a way she had never seen them before. An unwanted idea took hold of her mind. She spoke it to Thyripolis: 'I'm heading for something dark, aren't I, really dark? But you will be somewhere near? That's it, isn't it?'

His eyes said yes.

CHAPTER 10

CLUES FROM THE CITADEL

As Beth and Thyripolis reached the final sentry point at the top of the hill, she stared up at the grand entrance to the Citadel. It was far bigger than it looked from the town – a fortress with towers, fine windows and wide arches. Suddenly, Thyripolis flew off high over the town, heading to the hill beyond Boarham towards the sea. Her eye caught a tiny brilliant light shining on the horizon. Was that his destination?

She followed him longingly, hanging on to her belief that his going, for whatever reason, was part of a bigger plan than she could understand. But she felt painfully alone and empty. Except… she sniffed… a log fire? Could that be—

'You! Over there!' shouted an armed gatekeeper. 'What do you want?'

She moved to his hut and, as boldly as she could, explained, 'I'm from Mr Pinwell's Bakery – an urgent delivery.'

His sharp eyes assessed her, then silently, he held out an open hand. She presented her pass. He looked at her sternly. 'Number three's missing.'

'Please, Sir, the sentry—'

'Wasn't there?'

She nodded.

'He's always missing, bother him! It's his gumtuminous leg, or so he claims. Hmm. Go over there. Look for the small door of the Enquiry and Interrogations Office. Ask for more instructions. Remember to say, "Fools like me," when they ask what Lord Tresquin hates most.'

He directed her through the Citadel's main arch, past an enormous golden Boar, to the far side of a large courtyard. After the office had opened its tiny speaking window and accepted her code-words, she was dismissed with: 'The cakes go to the Small Boardroom above the Combat Chamber in Strangers Tower.' She managed to ask the way from a passing stable-boy and, on arrival, pushed open its heavy door.

In the tower's echoing grey hallway, she saw a rough notice: 'Stonemay Sons Progess Meating, Bored Room Second Flor.' It was signed 'VP'. While reading it, Beth felt that someone was staring at her, but when she looked up, it was only another painting of Lord Tresquin. She stared at it. Something was odd. The face? The narrow eyes? That was it – the eyes. They were different colours: one was blue and the other brown. Odd. A sound of cheering from above shook her back to her mission and she darted up to the second floor.

Her heart was already pounding, but it thumped violently as she reached the boardroom. From the voices inside, it sounded full. She hesitated, then knocked hard on the door. The muffled talking on the other side stopped at once. A calm, powerful voice spoke up: 'Gentlemen, please don't be alarmed. This is likely to be our cakes. At last. We will take a short break.' A rumble of lively conversation began.

The door was unlocked by a thin-faced man, smartly dressed in red. He spoke to Beth as though he was looking down on a dirty stray cat: 'The cakes are welcome, if four and a half minutes late.' His voice was oily. 'Baked by Mr Pinwell himself, can you confirm?'

'Yes, Sir. They're quite fresh.'

'Of course. Mr Pinwell would know what would happen to him if they weren't.'

Beth bowed her head, not just to play the servant, but also to look round the room as fast as she could for clues. A chart was on display at the front, but she was at the wrong angle to see it properly. Nothing else looked promising. Though she felt the stares of everyone in the meeting, another part of her brain was trying hard to identify the leader's voice. Surely she had heard it before, but she had never met anyone like this.

'Put the cakes on the plates over there by the window,' he continued, 'then take them to these important gentlemen.'

Beth wondered why this odd mixture of men was considered important. No two were the same in age or size, and their clothes ranged from rough to elegant.

'It would be very unfortunate if you dropped any, you know,' added the leader with a mocking voice.

Beth crossed carefully to the other side of the panelled room and started setting out the cakes. *Keep playing your part*, she repeated to herself. Her acting skills had never felt more important.

'Gentlemen, gentlemen... Thank you. We will be served cakes by Miss... er...' He waved his hand dismissively in Beth's direction, not bothering with a name. 'Perhaps while she does so, we could continue our discussion about *the canal*. You may find the chart helpful.'

The important gentlemen seemed surprised at the topic their leader had suggested. They stared at the chart blankly but found little to say about canals. What jolted Beth, almost dropping her plates, was catching sight of what they were looking at. It was the same as the map they had studied with Sash at Woollie, Haddock and Cringe, but it had many more crosses on it. A pain shot over her like a cold shower, but she had to move on quickly to avoid being caught staring at the chart. She returned to the cakes and finished serving.

Then, with her head spinning, she excused herself with a simple, 'Thank you, Sir.'

Without a word, the leader hurried her out and watched her go back to the staircase. After three steps down, the door was closed and locked. She checked that no one was in sight, then crept back to the room to fix Joe's bugging device into the keyhole. Thankfully a noisy discussion was underway inside.

From the RAT she chose a key that looked the best fit for the lock. She pushed it in as silently as she could, but it wouldn't go. She tried again with more force. Still stuck. The leader's key was blocking the hole from the other side. With a silent sigh of frustration, she stepped back to study the doorway. How else could she deploy the keys on the RAT? She spotted a gap under the door. Would they fit? She spread the keys out, making them flat enough to slide in gently, leaving the fob-switch outside for her to turn on. With the raised voices in the meeting, no one had noticed. She hid in the corridor around a corner, well out of sight. The earpiece of her RAT fitted perfectly and was easy to cover by letting her hair down. Clear voices came through – great reception!

The leader was talking again: 'So far, we have done well.' His voice sharpened. 'But *not* well enough. We are behind the Lord's schedule and he is... upset. The final deadline is close, and he demands we do better. You will see from the chart that we have made good strikes in Caladrin and Boarham. But have we treated every one of their so-called leaders? No! Lord Tresquin insists that we put them all on the bridge or show them in the Main Square – by tomorrow night. And, yes, you will need to use a high first dose for all. Stanton – you will be responsible for this. If you fail, you know that the Well awaits you.'

Beth *had* heard this voice before, but where?

'Fortunately,' the leader continued, 'we have good supplies of *Coagulosolidum*, thanks to Mr Haddock. That's right, Doctor, isn't it?' Beth heard a faint noise in reply.

'Good. At least something is working. We can use this batch in many different forms: liquid, powder, spray, soap, medicines – however you can best disguise it…

'Which reminds me…' Here, for once, he sounded genuinely pleased. '…the spray worked to perfection yesterday with Mrs Goodseed… well… after we had jangled her a little. *So* rewarding! It was a simple routine *I* invented of using a beautifully scented "insect spray" for a non-existent insect – well, in this case a cockroach. I gave such a big dose, too. The changes will happen very quickly. Mr Chelkwyn, you might need to call round sooner than usual to see if the lady is… ready.

'I used the usual protection, of course.' The leader's voice became low and serious. 'Gentleman, you must *always* pay attention to that. Stay… *safe*. Otherwise, sadly, we lose you from the Lord's Stonemasons – and what's more, we waste our poison. We import the antidote at high cost, so do treat it carefully. And remember, if it gets into the "patient", it can completely undo our effective poisoning.'

Beth's brain was alight with anger and questions. She had recognised the voice; it was Atticus Grobe – or whatever he was really called. 'Mrs Goodseed' must be Granelda, and he had poisoned her the day before, a few feet in front of her. She had little time to take this in before her earpiece emitted a deep rasping noise. Atticus had opened the door, which had scraped the RAT-keys across the stone floor. She held on to her receiving ear for a moment, then made sure it was well covered by her hair and cap. She tried to hide as best she could by flattening herself against the wall.

Atticus had the keys in his hand and was addressing his fellow Stonemasons from the doorway: 'Gentlemen, I pray you would join me in a search for the owner of this most unusual bunch of keys. He – or perhaps *she* – must be missing them. They should be returned. So *useful!*'

It didn't take them long to find Beth. She had nowhere to go. Her corridor was a dead end and all its doors were locked. Two important gentlemen were blocking the stairs.

Atticus dragged Beth into the middle of the gathering. 'Ah, Miss... er...?' he began in his most sinister voice.

'Hayfield. Meanda Hayfield.'

'Charming! That has *such* a nice ring. So have *these...*' He held up the keys and jangled them. 'A *very* curious design. Perhaps quite valuable? They are yours, aren't they?'

Beth gave the tiniest of nods.

'You dropped them on the way out, I expect?'

'Yes. Yes, I suppose I did.'

'No. No, you didn't. I watched you very carefully as you left.' Sharp anger swelled up in his voice. 'You insolent child! I don't know what you have to do with Mr and Mrs Pinwell – we'll visit them anyway – but I sense mischief, possibly… *spying*…' He bent down to speak close to her face: '…which, in the middle of the Citadel, is, you might understand, quite wrong. *Very* wrong. Now, for men who spy on us, execution or the Well is usual. But we do have this silly business of the law having to agree the same punishment for a child, especially a girl, even if they are obviously guilty. Then again, I am sure Lord Tresquin would see the need in this case.

'Convicts usually get a good audience. So, you gutter-child, you might be famous for a short time while the crowds watch you die. But then forgotten. As you should be.'

Something gave Beth the strength to look her accuser in the eye all the time he spoke.

'Unfortunately,' the leader continued, 'the prison cells in the Citadel are full. Traitors against the Lord, you know – so *many* these days. We will have to take you to the "Paupers' Lock-up" next to the River Gate. It's less… *cosy*, but everyone passing by can greet you – one way or another. A trial to prove the case will be necessary – but just a formality. Vacuus, would you please get the cage?'

Vacuus knew exactly what to do. His previous foolishness had vanished. Beth was bundled roughly down the stairs and locked into a small metal cage on wheels. It was filthy inside and smelled horribly like drains. She was jolted down the winding path towards the town, sometimes getting so close to the edge that she was certain she would topple over. As she passed the sentries, some jeered, some ignored her. One gave her a thumbs-down, another, a kindly look. Her eyes were watering from the cold wind. She could think of Thyripolis – but only in black and far away. Ever since she had arrived at the Citadel the scent of a log fire had lingered faintly in her nose, but now the awful stench of the cage swamped it completely. She had never felt so useless or alone.

As soon as the cage lurched through the city gate, crowds gathered round. They always peered at Lord Tresquin's latest prisoners. Who was it? What had they done wrong, if anything? A few mothers looked sad, but most had seen children like this a dozen times and had grown hardened to the sight. Staring faces in the Square surrounded her. Children stuck their tongues out and shouted silly names. Someone offered to give Beth a drink and for a moment she felt her spirits lift. She propped herself up ready to receive it, but then the someone simply threw cold water over her head and laughed. Beth sank back to the cage floor and shut her wet eyes. Was Joe anywhere nearby?

Until the cage and the commotion came by, Joe had been wandering round the Square eavesdropping for clues – but with no success. Hearing the noise, he pushed forward to see what was happening. His heart went out to the child curled up on the cage floor, wet and sobbing. What must she have done to deserve that? When he realised it was Beth his muscles turned to jelly and an echoing noise tore his brain apart.

'Beth! *Beth!*' He tried to shout but his voice was weak. He couldn't move an inch, never mind battle through the crowd. The cage and the throng of jeering faces jostled down towards the River Gate. He *must* move. He must reach Beth to let her know he was there, that he had seen her in this ghastly procession.

Adrenaline took over. He ran and pushed his way forwards but could not get close. Beth was being thrown into a small, dingy prison cell built into the city wall near its gate. He called out and tried to wave, but she sank straightaway into the rough straw that covered the stone floor. Behind the bars, she turned towards the far wall and covered her face. The metal door clanged shut. Keys rattled. A guard turned the lock.

Keys! The listening keys, thought Joe. Had Beth been caught at a keyhole? Was she still wearing the RAT's earpiece?

He ran back to the bakery faster than he had ever run before.

'Excuse me… Mrs Pinwell.' He was hardly able to speak. 'Can I… squeeze past? I need my coat… in Mr Pinwell's snug.'

'You're in a bad state, Joe,' she replied. 'What's wrong?'

'Beth! She's in prison! I'll tell you more in a minute… I need to… Thanks.'

Mrs Pinwell had unlocked the snug door. 'He doesn't usually let anyone in here alone,' she said.

Joe rushed past her anyway. He grabbed his coat and from his OAK took out a small oblong box. *Click.* He spoke into it urgently: 'Beth! Beth! I'm in the bakery. I've seen where they've taken you. We'll bring you some food and get you out really soon. I'll work on it with Mr Pinwell and Mr Cringe. If you can hear me in your earpiece, take it out. Try using it as a microphone. It might get through. But don't get yourself into trouble.'

He took a breath and waited.

Silence. Crackles. Silence again. Rustling. Then a faint, whispered, 'Joe! Yes… I'm—'

Thumping sounds replaced Beth's voice, then nothing.

Mr and Mrs Pinwell strode in and demanded to know what was happening. In a torrent of words, Joe explained.

'I knew using this "apparatus" would bring trouble,' said Mrs Pinwell. 'Old-fashioned gossip, that's what I recommended. But children always want something new and fancy. Bound to bring disaster.'

'Nightmare!' said Mr Pinwell. 'Shouldn't have done it.'

'Can I take her some food?' asked Joe. 'And how can we get her out?'

'Food?' said the baker. 'If she gets water, she'll be better off than most prisoners. Mrs Pinwell could take some bread after dark. Might work – with bribery. Get her out with a guard watching? Need to believe the impossible for that. Better go back to Mr Cringe for ideas. Can't hang around Beth, either. Too much friendly interest and you'll be in prison with her. Go back to the Manufactory through the west gate. Find the Cringes' house.'

'Have a chocolate truffle for the journey,' offered Mrs Pinwell.

Most townspeople passing Beth's cell ignored her, though a few stopped for a moment out of curiosity or pity. She slumped on the floor looking at a damp stone wall away from her spectators. She knew Joe and Mr Cringe would do all they could to help, but what power had they against Lord Tresquin's soldiers and the poisonous Stonemasons?

Someone had spoken to her recently about help. The events of the past few days tumbled through her head. It was… Granelda… about Thyripolis… *'Don't forget you can call on him for help; it will come at the right time even if you can't understand it.'* Beth tried hard to think of his shimmering colours and piercing eyes and to imagine those rainbow scents. Against the evil smell of her dingy prison, it wasn't easy. Her lips moved silently as she called, 'Thyripolis, please come! Please help! We've more to do here, haven't we, even if we haven't done very well yet? Don't let this be the end of our journey. *Please.'*

Nothing changed.

Weakness spread over her. Her mind switched off. She sank into the powdery straw and fell asleep.

When she woke up, the moon was shining through a high window. It had no glass – just a square opening in the wall narrowed by two vertical bars. Looking silvery in the moonlight, misty night air drifted into her cell. It was bitterly cold. Close to her cell, outside her prison bars, a guard was sitting at a small table writing sleepily in a book by the light of an oil lamp.

A rustling sound came from the straw in the corner. Beth's challenge was not to scream. If spiders were agony – rats were death! She stood up and held on to the iron bars as far away from the noise as possible. All went quiet, but her eyes stayed glued to the suspicious corner. The straw began to move. She gripped the bars harder. No animal appeared, but the straw along the wall under the window was growing upwards. She braved a closer look then tried stepping on it. It held her weight. A tiny squeak above made her look up towards the window. There was nothing new to be seen, but it made her wonder whether she could escape by squeezing on her side between its vertical bars. She could try, but for two problems: the window was still out of reach and the guard would spot her easily.

Voices from the guard's table made her look round. Mrs Pinwell had brought food and was pleading with the guard to give it to the prisoner. He refused, as expected. An argument broke out. A bribe was offered, but it wasn't enough. Beth looked up at the window. It was closer than before. She looked down and saw that the straw had grown higher, taking her with it. But she was not yet high enough to chance an escape.

Mrs Pinwell offered more money. This time it was enough. The guard stood up quickly, grabbing at the coins and the bread. But doing so, he knocked against the table. The oil lamp fell off and as it hit the stone floor, its glass chimney shattered.

The shouts between the guard and Mrs Pinwell gave Beth the cover she needed to escape – but she was still too far from the window. She tried to gain height by thrusting down her right leg – but she hardly moved.

The spilt oil caught fire and trickled under the bars of the cell, setting light to the dry straw. The guard and Mrs Pinwell stopped fighting and began a desperate search for water. The fire bucket was empty. Mrs Pinwell poured Beth's drink on the burning straw, but it did nothing to slow the advancing flames. The guard rushed back to a sentry point in the main square to raise an alarm. The only key that would unlock the cell went with him.

Mrs Pinwell stared with horror as she saw the fire moving towards Beth. Seeing her high on a pile of dry straw, ready for burning, all she could do was shout frantically: 'Beth! Look! The flames are nearly underneath you. *Quick!* Can you get through the window – hang on the outside somehow? Oh! The poor girl!'

In spite of her danger, Beth found a surprising sense sweep over her – a calm determination to escape whatever it took. To her, the fire was 'down there'. The moonlight lit up the silvery mist and a smell of pine forests swirled round her as though she was in a different world. Not that she stayed where she was. Looking at the wall just above her, she saw a possible foothold – a rusty iron hoop. Instantly, with all her energy, she pushed herself up, twisted sideways and thrust one arm between the window bars. She made herself as flat as possible. Then, by pulling and pushing with both arms, she managed to get her head and shoulders right through. By now, her legs were catching the intense heat of the flames and smoke was drifting through the window. Groping desperately over the wall outside, she found a bracket with a pulley within reach above her. Using both arms, she grabbed hold of it and pulled the rest of her body clear. She was out – hanging above the river.

A moment later, smoke began pouring through the window. Her eyes watered and stung with pain. She started coughing. Every part of her shouted that she couldn't hold on for much longer. The flames reached the window, licking its edges. She glanced down but could see nothing. The moon had clouded over, and her stinging eyes wouldn't open. Her fingers were losing their grip. She had to let go.

CHAPTER 11

A RIDDLE OF HOPE

Beth shrieked as she hit the cold, dark water of the river – and sank. Her feet squelched into the mud at the bottom. For a moment she was stuck. Then, fighting with all her limbs, she got free, spluttered to the surface and began to swim.

The moon was shining again but showed no easy place for her to climb onto the bank. The current carried her towards the centre of the river and beyond the bridge. When she looked back for a moment, she saw flames and smoke still shooting out from the prison window. Then she saw the statues. The cold moon was lighting up their deathly faces, sharpening the lines of their pain. How soon would Merrin and Granelda join them…?

In the silence, she heard a faint sound of splashing. Just as she looked downstream, a brilliant light flashed towards her. Should she call out? Answer: her voice was too weak with coughing to make enough noise anyway. The splashing got louder. The light wobbled. It was getting closer.

Someone shouted: 'Beth! It's us! Paddling powerfully in pursuit of your protection!' It had to be Sash.

Joe was in the boat, too. He switched off his PEST and together they pulled Beth aboard.

'Keep low,' he whispered. 'Lie down if you can. Back to the jetty at full speed!' While they were underway, Joe asked Beth how she managed to escape.

'Squeezed through the window and dropped into the river,' said Beth in a husky voice.

'That easy…?'

'A raging fire in the prison cell spurred me on.'

'Peril! Perfect peril!' said Sash.

'What made you come?' asked Beth.

'No particular plan – just proximity, perchance to perceive any possibilities,' said Sash.

Joe translated: 'Sash was keen to get closer to the prison in case there was something we could do. We borrowed a boat from the landing stage at the Manufactory. He thought his father wouldn't mind.'

In a short while they moored the boat back where it belonged and found their way to the Cringes' kitchen. Joe lit a candle, Sash found a rug to wrap round Beth and all three sat round the table. Leftover pieces of bread were scrounged from a plate nearby and Sash found a lump of cheese under a dry cloth. Beth rescued a raw carrot that had fallen on the floor. Together, they ate this grand spread while Beth told them more about Mrs Pinwell's visit and what had happened next.

'Proliferating pear trees! That was a narrow escape!' said Sash. 'I must propel a wiff pronto to the bakery to say you are preserved. They'll be paralysed with perplexity. Pardon me!' He disappeared into the darkness towards Mr Haddock's menagerie.

Beth shared what she had found out from the Citadel.

'Mr Pinwell was right,' she said. 'It's not a curse, it's a poison. It can be given in lots of different ways… And it's been given to Granelda.'

'*Granelda?*' said Joe. 'How could anyone do that? How was it done? It's not our fault, is it?' he added with a look of horror.

'No. It was those slimy imposters who pushed their way in to Granelda's kitchen. They pretended to see a cockroach on her head. The one who called himself "Atticus" sprayed their "anti-cockroach potion" over her head and face. That was the poison. It happened right in front us, but from our hideouts, we couldn't see it.'

'How did you find out?'

'Merrin. She saw it all and told us afterwards. We didn't know it was a poison at the time. Granelda even enjoyed its "lovely smell". Yesterday, when I took cakes to the Citadel, I met Atticus. He was in charge of the meeting. Through your RAT I could hear him tell his "important gentlemen" all about poisoning the Archers. Then he boasted of his trick to use the cockroach-spray on a "Mrs Goodseed" – Granelda.'

Joe put his hands in the air and mimed wringing Mr Grobe's neck. 'I hate him! I hate him! Can't we poison *him*?'

'No. We've got to keep our heads down and find out how this is all planned. Lord Tresquin *has* to be behind it, but who are his puppets – apart from this hateful pair?'

'What can we do?'

'I don't know... But I'll tell you what else I heard: Mr Haddock is supplying the poison.'

'Really? Old maggot-face? Who would believe that?'

'And it was Mr Chelkwyn who poisoned Merrin.'

'Mr Chelkwyn? I can't remember him.'

'But, listen, Joe – here's the real break-through! There *is* an antidote that protects against the poison and can restore its victims back to normal!'

'That's... interesting...'

'Joe, you're not hearing me!' said Beth. 'We've found an anti—'

'Water. I am hearing dripping water. Can you hear it?'

'No. Where?'

'Underneath me?'

'Really?'

Drops were falling from the chair to the floor.

'It's you!' said Beth.

'Me? I'm not wet.'

'Near the side of your breeches…'

Joe felt around. His pocket was soaking, the pocket with the *Guide* in it. The *Guide. Again…* Now what? He pulled it out. Water ran from between its pages and splashed onto his hand.

'Another clue?' said Beth. 'We could do with that.'

Joe played it cool. Though curious, he was still annoyed by this thing that couldn't really exist. He held the book up to the candle and opened it where the water was trickling out. After a gush came a gentle flow; then it stopped altogether.

'Let's see,' said Beth.

They both looked into a clear pond with a few reeds. Underneath the water lay a mass of tiny pebbles.

'Maybe the answer is in those,' said Beth.

Joe looked again. 'There is a shape to them, I think.'

Using the Omniscope in *Close-up* mode and a daylight beam from his PEST, he read the words that were spelt out in lines of dark-coloured stones:

Yellow leads to white;
You've already seen the sight.
Purple leads to pink,
But for this you'll have to sink.

'What yellow leads to what white? Your bakery dress is a muddy sort of yellow and the Citadel dome is nearly white. Is this about your expedition there?' asked Joe.

'Maybe, but we've got clues from there already: Atticus and his spray... his... *yellow* spray! That's what Merrin said. That's the "yellow". It must be. The yellow poison.'

'Good connection,' said Joe. 'So, the "white" must be the marble statues.'

'Of course! You saw the statues on the bridge... And that's why Granelda was much paler yesterday morning – and really irritable at breakfast. The poison was already taking hold.'

'Scum! She might have been all frilly and pot plants, but she was kind and made great soup. She trusted us to help...' sighed Joe. 'Not much use so far, are we? I can't compute the purple.'

'We are getting *somewhere*,' said Beth. 'We still have a mission. Loads of people are still in danger – and *listen* – there *is* an antidote!'

'Where? What is it?'

'I don't know. Can we get more help to find out?'

'From whom? The beautiful bakers? I don't think they've got any more jam in their doughnuts.'

'What about Mr Cringe?' suggested Beth. 'He seems a good egg. There's always the possibility of—'

'Please don't mention the *bird*... We've got to work this out *logically*.'

Beth looked sad. If only Joe could see...

'Let's go to bed. I need my sleep to get the right sort of brain waves for this. We'll consult Jarek – sorry, Mr Cringe, Sir, tomorrow.'

On their way to breakfast, Beth wondered if they should mention the news about Mr Haddock. Joe disagreed, wanting more evidence before they spoke up. Good smells drew them into the kitchen where they joined the Cringe family for Ossabaw hog bacon, poached eggs and thick slices of toast.

'Beth! You're back! Wonderful! Whatever happened?' asked Mr Cringe with an almost luminous face. 'Feed her up well, Mrs Cringe. She looks in fine need of sustenance.'

'A profound pleasure to see you!' said Sash, his mouth broadcasting more toast crumbs than words.

While the Ravens told their stories between mouthfuls of breakfast and gulps of juice, Mr Cringe asked little. At the end he congratulated them both on all they had achieved.

'What a prestigious pair!' said Sash. 'I'm so proud. What progress! What a performance!'

Mr Cringe continued: 'So... a yellow poison that twists the mind and then makes its victims rock solid. What would do that?'

In a blink, Joe had an idea: 'Something that precipitates intracellular calcium as an insoluble salt,' said Joe. 'Nerves, muscles and the heart would be really sensitive to that.'

'That's all beyond me, Joe,' said Mr Cringe. 'But thanks – it strengthens our case.'

'Impermeable,' muttered Sash.

'Whatever else we do,' continued Mr Cringe, 'we must warn all our Archers right now to keep out of contact with anything yellow, unless they know exactly where it's from. Sash, can you organise urgent messages and the wiffs to take them? Use the Post-clock service, too. Take care! The spies of Lord Tresquin will be out in force.'

'Certainly, Father. A prescient plan.'

Sash sped away, trailing more remnants of his hearty breakfast.

'I have a thought,' said Mr Cringe. 'This evil man, Atticus, and his not-so-dim friend must have breathed in some of their spray, yet they weren't worried about the poison. How did that work?'

Beth spoke about Atticus, in his meeting, warning the important gentlemen of their need for protection: 'They use something that's imported, but not through your Manufactory.' She thought back to Granelda's kitchen when the imposers called. 'This may have nothing to do with it, but Atticus and his stooge had a drink before they sprayed Granelda. "Blueberry and onion squash", they called it. Merrin told me later about a drop they spilt on the floor. She said it smelt more like fish than fruit. I guess it's still there.'

'Let's go and see,' said Joe, already starting to move.

'Whoa…' said Mr Cringe, holding up his hand. 'Let me propose a plan: we will take you the Boarham jetty. Can you find your way to Granelda's house from there?'

Beth nodded.

'See how Granelda is,' continued Mr Cringe, 'and try to get a sample of the spilt drink. Then at twelve o'clock, catch the Mail Coach that stops near Mrs

Maggutt's general shop. It will be going to Caladrin, but on the way, it calls at the house of Dr McFudgett. You must talk to him. Show him what you have found. He's a brilliant thinker and cares a lot about our problem.'

'Sash told me about him – and his balloon,' said Joe. 'Is he an Archer, too? Should we tell him about the "no-yellow" rule?'

'Yes, of course – we must. He might be able to spread the message, too. He's not an *official* Archer, but he's been a grand help to us once or twice. He is well known to our group, though he's busy with his experiments most of the time. He keeps out of town life – concentrates on his "philosophical enquiries".'

Joe glowed with delight. 'I'll get my OAK. He might like to see what I've made.'

Beth looked hard at him and mouthed the word, 'Careful,' to remind him of Granelda's warning not to reveal their real background. Joe frowned and disappeared with, 'I'll get my kit anyway.'

With everything ready, they took a pony and trap crossing over the Caladrin bridge to reach Granelda's cottage in Boarham. When they arrived outside Quince Cottages, everything looked just as before, though there was an air of heaviness that they neither expected nor liked. Beth and Joe went straight to the front door and knocked hard. As expected, there was no answer.

'Hello!' shouted Beth through the keyhole.

'Go away! No visitors!' Granelda's voice was weak and slow.

'It's us – Joe and Beth. Can we come in?'

'Come round the back if you must.'

Inside, the kitchen was a mess. No fire warmed the room. The smell of tasty food had become stale. Granelda's face was pale and hard, and she was moving stiffly. 'Well? Have you anything useful to say?'

Beth began: 'We've found out that the yellow "cockroach spray" was really a poison.' She paused. 'We hate those terrible salesmen who squirted you with it. We're really sor –'

'That's *it*? You must feel clever! Or was it Mr Cringe's brainwave?'

'Merrin and I had already worked that out – and that Mr Chelkwyn's "golden liquid" was the same.'

Joe took over: 'We're on the track of a *cure* – the drink that they had before using the poison. Merrin said that some of it spilled on the floor. We've come to see if we can look at it – maybe take a sample…'

'Thank you *so* much for coming to see if *I* was all right. Still, I know live specimens are always in short supply, and I am thrilled to help you with your experiments, Joe. Not that I will be a live specimen for long. Do help yourself to my floor. I can't get down to clean it, so the mark is still there. I'm going to the sitting room. By the way, the curse is more than a poison.'

In pain, she moved slowly. As she went, Beth called out, 'How is Merrin?'

'Nearly dead. You will soon see us both on Caladrin bridge or the Boarham Hall Drive. But thank you *so* much for your help.'

'Let's get on with it, Beth,' whispered Joe urgently. 'Time is against us.'

'I know.'

They found the small mark of the spilt drink.

'Look – it's purple,' said Beth. 'The other colour in our riddle.'

'...and purple leads to pink,' said Joe. 'This is the antidote! It must be!'

'Can Dr McFudgett prove it?'

'Let's take him some.'

Joe poured water onto the spot to dissolve it.

'Jammed cogs!' he said. 'We need a pipette and a small bottle for the sample.'

'How about the convenience store?' suggested Beth.

Thinking hard about the items they needed, Joe approached it not knowing what to expect. First it produced a very small fruit pip and a bottle fly; but the second time it delivered the goods required. A small sample of purple solution was collected successfully, and, as Granelda had fallen asleep, they crept away to catch the coach outside Mrs Maggutt's store.

CHAPTER 12

THE SIGNPOST

Travelling in the Mail Coach was like being pushed in a wheelbarrow with a square wheel. Its springs did little to smooth the bumps in the road. As it crunched over potholes and rocks, Beth and Joe were jolted in all directions.

'What do you think he'll be like?' said Beth.

'Dr McFudgett? Mr Cringe thinks he's very clever and helpful. Sash says he's forever trying out new ideas. He's probably friendly, though a bit stormy, I guess. Oh, and he likes to eat girls on Thursdays.'

'He'll find me tough,' said Beth.

The coach juddered over a stone.

'I wonder what he does with the frogs,' said Beth.

'Aha,' said Joe, his face looking wild. 'Bashes their

heads in, then cuts them up for experiments – like this.' His eyes narrowed while he pretended to cut into Beth's hand.

'Go away!' she said. Then, 'Hey, this is wobbly.'

They were both being thrown from side to side.

BANG! The carriage tilted sharply, shot round in a circle and stopped dead. Beth landed in a corner on top of Joe. A shout came from the Post Office Guard as he climbed to the ground. The horses reared up with shrieks of alarm.

'That's a wheel gone,' said Joe in a squashed voice.

The boy driver jumped down to inspect the damage. What came next was probably an eighteenth-century swear-word. Then he remembered he had two passengers on board to help.

'Sorry 'bout that,' said the boy. ''Appens sometimes. Should've checked it 'fore I set off. Anyway, that's yer journey ended in this thing, an' prob'ly the end of me as well. People 'ate getting their post late… or not at all. The Guard'll be furious. Yer going to the doctor's 'ouse, aren't yer? Well, you could wait 'ere fer the next coach tomorro', or try walkin'. Don't look like yer've got much to carry an' it ain't more than a few miles if yer know yer way.'

'We'll walk,' said Beth. Joe nodded without any enthusiasm.

'Well, keep goin' on this road, then over the 'ill, take the right fork. The doctor's put a signpost some place up there. That'll 'elp. But watch yerselves if the ground gets soggy. Yer can get mighty stuck in it. An' if yer taking the top path, there's nasty brambles nearby that yer'd better not get stung by. Wha'ever bit of yer they stick in dies off.'

'I wonder how that happens,' said Joe, mostly to himself.

'I'll un'itch the 'orses and sort out with the Guard what's to do. I'll 'ave to ride back to the Post Office with the bags anyway. I guess it's me lookin' for another job after that. Some 'ope! 'Ere, 'ave these for yer journey,' he grunted. The boy handed over a few boiled sweets. They were partly wrapped in scruffy paper and looked as though they had once been dropped in mud.

'Great!' said Beth, with pretend enthusiasm. 'What's your name, by the way?'

'Pip. Yer know, Pip at the Post... Ha. No more, I reckon. Bye! Good luck!'

Pip and the Guard burst into a furious argument while Beth and Joe started walking.

The uneven track rose steadily uphill. Joe was pleased to have his coat, mostly because of his OAK in his pocket. It had been missing for far too long. The coat itself was heavy: hot to carry and even hotter to put on. At last, when the hill flattened, they could see the right-hand fork, the one that Pip had explained. They could also make out the top of the signpost. With aching legs they turned downhill; their energy was draining away in the high sun.

'Let's make it to the signpost,' said Beth, 'then have a rest.'

'So says our leader!' proclaimed Joe. 'And we all say, "What a great plan!"'

The signpost was stuck in a small grassy mound. At its top was an ornamental shape looking like an onion. Two arms showed the possible ways they could go. One pointed straight ahead where the road looked good; the other pointed to the right, where a rotting gate led into rising woodland covered in undergrowth. The writing on both arms had long since blurred into the decaying wood and was hard to read.

Beth took a closer look. 'Funny,' she said. 'I think *both* arms say "To Dodgison House". That's Dr McFudgett's place, isn't it?'

'Yes. I'll check the image-analysis app on my Omniscope,' said Joe. From his pocket, he took a small, irregular tube with a lens at one end, an eyepiece at the other, a variety of buttons and a small screen.

He dictated to the machine: 'Alpha-numeric analysis and comparison: distance, twenty; images, two. Go!' He pointed it at each arm of the signpost in turn.

The data were analysed in a few seconds. The Omniscope announced, 'Answer: Concordance = 97%. Dodgison House confirmed.'

Joe looked through the lens at the full analysis. 'They both say what you thought. So, either direction would take us to Dr McFudgett's house.'

'I don't mind which way we go,' said Beth, 'though the woodland route looks tough going. Why don't we rest on this bank before setting off?' In true acting style, she added, 'My whole frame aches with weariness. My scorched feet and burnt head cry out for relief. Even my heart is parched, straining with every beat.'

'A bit tired then?'

The plan was agreed to have a ten-minute break, then use Joe's Random Allocation Number Generator (RANG) to choose which path to take. Resting in the sun in this peaceful spot, they both made themselves comfortable and thought silently about the previous twenty-four hours.

'Stop it!' said Beth.

'What?'

'Tickling me.'

'I wasn't.'

'Yes, you were!'

'No. I'm just resting and thinking.'

'So, please stop tickling me!'

'Beth, I am *not*. Hey! You don't have to tickle *me* when I've done nothing!'

'I'm *not!*'

'Yes, you *are!*'

'But you're laughing.'

'Beth Raven, I… am… *not!*'

'Oh, what fun!' said a deep, chuckling voice above them. 'It was me all the time!'

A face, wrinkled with laughter, had appeared on the signpost's 'onion'. Its arms, elongated for the purpose, were doing the tickling. Given their adventures so far, Beth and Joe were hardly surprised at what was happening; but they did complain that the signpost had seriously disturbed their rest.

'I am *so* sorry about that,' said the signpost. 'I *do* like to be helpful. I saw that you found it difficult to read my arms and that you have not yet decided which route to take. Now, what can I best advise? I make it a habit to inspect all the routes I point to before making a recommendation.'

The signpost jumped out of the ground and stood on two small legs. In the strange world they now inhabited, Beth and Joe accepted even this with little surprise.

'Well… across the road, we have the *Country Route*. It's overgrown with brambles, bindweed and cacti – all extremely dangerous in their own way. You would need to take great care. Beyond that, the path is a slippery one. It goes sharply up to top of the hill behind Dr McFudgett's house. That would give you a *wonderful* view of his estate. It's in a disused quarry. Do come and have a look.'

The signpost ran across the road and pointed out the direction of the weed-covered path. Beth and Joe stayed to watch from where they were.

'*Or*,' he said, wandering back to his mound, 'the *Official Route* offers a *much* better road. It goes directly downhill. It's wide, smooth and clutter-free, and it would be considerably quicker. You'll only see the *front* of Dr McFudgett's residence, though, and before you get there you may meet a boggy patch where the road can get impassable. I haven't been down that way recently, but we've had no rain for at least a day.' He sounded encouraging.

The signpost jumped back into his hole and looked seriously at both children. 'There you have it: the latest travel information from our worldwide company, Signs – Your Life Away.'

'But which way would you *recommend?*' asked Joe.

'Ah… That is somewhat difficult, young man. The *Official Route* is more… acceptable, but occasionally there's a bit of, shall we say, bother, at the end. On the other arm, the *Country Route* is harder work and definitely not without risk. Though, you might well see something from there that proves important for your mission – whatever that is. You could always toss a coin.' He laughed. His chuckle lines returned – though they soon faded as the signpost returned to its usual shape.

Both children were irritable after this broken rest. They discussed the best way forward but clashed sharply over which route they should take. Joe made it clear that the 'official' route was far better: easier, quicker, safer and, well, *official*. Beth wanted to be more adventurous, especially as going the other way might give vital information for their task ahead. They could reach no agreement. Both were certain of being right. So, not in very good spirits, they each set off on their own way.

'A boiled sweet for whoever gets there first!' called out Beth, trying to ease the friction as they parted.

'Oh, how kind! But it's all right, Beth. I'll let *you* have one – as a booby prize.'

Beth crossed the road and quickly met her first obstacle: the broken gate at the entrance to the wood. She struggled to open it, succeeding only after a sharp kick. The path beyond was hidden by a mass of weeds and nettles. Brambles spread in front of her and bindweed was already catching at her feet.

Walking down the 'official' road (though it was still only a dusty track), Joe found just the opposite. It was comfortable, clear and safe underfoot. Gathering speed, he made good progress. It was easy to jog, and he often broke into a downhill run. He smiled at who would win the booby prize.

Beth battled painfully. She pushed back the brambles with a stick and so far had avoided catching herself on a thorn. Cacti appeared suddenly right in front of her. She leapt over them smartly to avoid injury, though when she looked back, they had disappeared.

As Joe reached halfway down the hill, a cloud drifted over the sun and a cool breeze began to blow in his face. He stopped to put on his coat and pull it tight. The sky turned black. Large drops of rain began to fall noisily on his head. He set off again at a faster pace, but the road under his feet grew sticky. Clumps of mud stuck to his shoes. The rain streaked down with increasing force. Lightning flashed in the distance and a rumble of thunder echoed across the valley below.

Beth was still in dappled sunshine. It was warm work, beating down the threatening undergrowth. Above the insect noises and birdsong, Beth heard an echoing whistle. It was curiously familiar. Her mind and muscles tensed. It must be Thyripolis. Her courage surged and, though she could not see him, his presence gave her energy to keep going. The matted weeds were still a challenge, but the trees were thinning out and the woodland getting lighter. Her silver bird called again – and she called back. She turned to look for him but caught her arm on a bramble.

Joe was finding it harder and harder to pull his feet out of the mud. His steps were achingly slow. Trying to lift one foot up made the other one sink more deeply. The storm was closing in on him. The lightning became frequent, followed almost instantly by the deepest thunder he had ever heard. Vibration from its roar rattled and gripped his chest. It was a fight for breath every time it rolled over him. Suddenly, his whole world exploded as intense jagged lightning struck a nearby clump of trees. He was blinded by its brilliance and deafened by the simultaneous violent crack of thunder. As it rolled away, it echoed around Joe's head while he struggled to take the next breath. Before the thunder had faded, its noise was overtaken by the crackling and low rumble of a raging fire advancing into the woodland. He was rigid and shivering. His legs sank further into the mud. He could not move at all. The more he tried to pull them out, the more the mud held on to him. Could the forest fire reach him across the wet ground? And the metallic gadgets in his pockets… wouldn't they be just right to attract the next flash of lightning?

A barb on the bramble had caught Beth's arm. Instant pain. Rubbing made no difference. Bleeding sores soon erupted round her punctured wound. The pain was getting worse, so she stopped rubbing. There was nothing else she could do. Around the sores, her skin was turning purple then forming a mass of white blisters. She sank onto a fallen tree, staring at the spread of the bramble's toxin.

Joe hoped so much that Beth could see him – but he knew that was impossible. The realisation pressed in on him that unless someone passed by, he was fixed. For good. And who would be out in this weather to look for him? He tried not to cry. *You're a failure!* jeered a voice in his head. *Called here to solve a problem brilliantly, and now you can't even move!* The rain lightened, though his cheeks stayed wet. The wind changed direction; it was swirling all round him, blowing in waves that made a strange sound.

Beth felt empty. It wouldn't be long before her arm would shrivel from the bramble's poison. If it spread further, her whole skin could look like slime. She might be completely unrecognisable, assuming Joe or somebody else could ever discover where she was. Suddenly she shouted at the trees, 'Why did Granelda bring us to Boarham if this is what was going to happen? Why? And Thyripolis – a wonderful present! Really? Just gives a whistle then disappears. Is that all he does?' She shouted again, though in her weakness, the sound was not at all loud. 'It's not enough, Granelda! You've lost us! We've los— *Ow!*' A blister on her arm burst open with a scalding pain and dripped murky green liquid onto her dress.

In her distress, she missed a swishing noise nearby. A bearded dragon, several feet long, had squeezed out between the roots of a gnarled tree. It was covered in silver scales. It looked like a lizard but had a head like a frog, with big eyes and a beard. As soon as it saw Beth, it stopped. But rather than run away in fright, it came over. It looked at her face, sniffed her hands, studied the spreading bramble bite – then slid away again. When it returned, one large hand carried two thistle heads, the other, a dark red fruit. It squeezed the juice from the fruit into the hollow of a nearby rock. Using the thistle heads, it painted the orange liquid, smelling of lemon, onto Beth's blistered arm.

'That's hot!' said Beth, holding her arm as still as possible. The animal looked at her with large dark eyes, hissed gently and continued the treatment.

The spinning waves of wind above Joe became intense. Caught up in this tornado, he began lifting out of the ground. Startled beyond belief, he was being carried in the air.

Beth's blistered skin healed quickly and she felt much better. After the animal had scurried away between the tree roots, she tried to sit up – but something very heavy fell down and knocked her over.

The tornado had dropped Joe next to the signpost. His landing was much softer than he expected. He had fallen on top of his sister.

'Get off!' cried Beth. 'I was… just… just… having a really strange dream.' She shook herself awake, pushed Joe away and sat up. She looked at her arm. It was perfectly normal.

Joe blinked hard in the sunshine and yawned. 'I had one too,' said Joe.

'I dreamt that the signpost came alive and pointed out the two ways we could get to Dr McFudgett's,' said Beth. 'I chose the *Country Route* but got poisoned by a bramble.'

'I had the same dream but took the *Official Route*.'

'I know.'

'I got completely stuck in deep mud when a huge thunderstorm set fire to the wood.'

Joe and Beth continued to share their dreams, then agreed to take the challenge of the woodland path.

'Let's get a good view of Dr McFudgett's estate before we meet him,' said Beth. 'That might be progress. Something tells me we'll find out a lot, *and* we'll be safe.'

'I'm not sure we can trust your "somethings"', said Joe.

CHAPTER 13

ROUND AT THE DOCTOR'S

Pushing through the real woodland was easier than in Beth's dream, but fallen tree trunks, hidden stones and slithery leaves made their journey slow.
'Mind the brambles!' said Beth, just in case.

Beyond the wood, an open hillside stretched up to the top of a quarry. Before climbing all the way, they stopped to look over its edge at Dr McFudgett's home.

'Wow!' said Joe. 'Buildings everywhere... and they're all round.'

'Well hidden, too,' said Beth.

As they scrabbled up higher, another round building came into view with a domed green roof of weathered copper. Joe and Beth battled against the wind to reach it just beyond the top of the quarry.

'It's an observatory,' said Joe. 'You can see the opening for the telescope. Dr McFudgett's, I guess. I wonder what's inside.'

He climbed up a small step and tried the brass door handle. '*Ouch!*' he cried, jumping sharply backwards. His EAR screeched from a high voltage charge. He rubbed his hand. 'Unfriendly, I'd say. A small "No Entry" sign would do.'

'Which, O inquisitive spirit, you would have treated with great respect, I know.'

'Every time.'

'Hey, look! Here's something else to engage the Great Mind.'

Beth had found what looked like a well with a high, glass roof. Its round brick wall surrounded a dark hole. A short ladder was fixed to the outside.

'Smells like the sea down there,' said Beth, peering inside. *What does that remind me of?*

'Let's see,' said Joe.

He leant over the wall and, using his PEST, set to *6K:70:10,* declared, 'No sea at the bottom – just dark stone. It's a long way down.'

Shining the bright beam round the walls higher up illuminated something much more interesting.

'There's a pulley system with a platform that almost reaches to the top,' he said. 'This must be how the Wonderful Philosopher gets lifted to see the stars.'

From the top of the quarry they could see the full extent of Dr McFudgett's estate. Dodgison House was a fine building near the road. It sprouted round towers of different sizes where you wouldn't expect them. Its courtyard held enormous wooden machines with ropes, pulleys and glass lenses. Behind it was a plant-filled garden enclosed by a high wall; beyond that, an enormous area with buildings of different sizes, all circular. In the middle of the site was a wide-open area with a raised platform. Large pipes from eight surrounding barrels led to its centre.

'That must be the launch-pad for Dr McFudgett's balloons,' said Joe, almost taking flight himself with excitement. 'I'd love to hitch a ride!'

'You'll be lucky!' said Beth. 'Not for me, thanks, unless we have to for the sake of our quest.'

Nearby was the biggest building of the collection, fixed against the quarry face itself. Another, close to it, was belching out smoke from a tall chimney and puffing steam from a shiny pipe lower down.

'Come on,' said Joe. 'Let's see the great man himself.'

They slithered down a thin path that skirted the quarry edge to reach a high-arched gate. There they pulled a heavy knob above the doctor's brass nameplate and waited for the wide black gates to open.

'Good afternoon, Beth. Good afternoon, Joe,' said a disembodied voice. 'Welcome to Dodgison House.' Dr McFudgett had appeared from nowhere and was standing behind them.

'Good afternoon, Sir,' said Beth.

Joe, distracted by guessing how the doctor had arrived, said the same – after a prod from his sister.

Dr McFudgett was surprisingly small, completely

round and full of colour. He wore an elegant bright red coat, a gold-patterned waistcoat, breeches and a frilly shirt. These were crowned by a white-powdered wig with a plaited tail encircled by a vivid green bow. He looked at his visitors through glasses so thick he seemed to have no eyes.

It was a short walk to his front door where he showed them into the hallway. Like him, it was small and completely round, but, in contrast, it was dark with heavy wooden panelling. Its only light came from a window in its domed ceiling.

'Welcome indeed! I have been expecting two young travellers,' he said warmly. 'How exciting to see you. I believe you like our new philosophical works, Joe? What do you think of *this*?' He showed them a model of the solar system set up in the centre of the room. Its planets and moons started moving.

'It's an orrery, Sir, isn't it?' said Joe. 'Driven by clockwork, I suppose?'

'Yes. It is… How clever of you!'

Did the doctor seem a little surprised that Joe knew the answer? It was spooky not being able to see his eyes.

Suddenly, the whole floor started rotating. Joe and Beth staggered to stay upright.

'Aha!' He smiled. 'A good effect, eh? It's a reminder that we are *all* spinning around the sun ourselves.'

After a couple of turns, the floor stopped moving. Dr McFudgett invited them into his 'elaboratory'. He opened the front door again, but this time it led into a large round room full of neatly arranged instruments.

Joe thought that if there really was a place called 'heaven', this is what it would be like. The walls were covered with astronomical charts while wooden gadgets with glass fronts and dials sat on numerous shelves waiting to be called into service. A giant prism projected a glorious rainbow on a measuring instrument of some sort. Joe also spotted a grandfather clock with a timetable on the side. Next to that was a tall cabinet of 'Animal Extracts' – jars of all colours labelled from 'Alligator' to 'Zebra'. A thin spidery tree was growing into the far end of the room, surrounded by a cage. Was that an animal inside?

'That's my chameleon, "Poly", said Dr McFudgett. 'Sometimes you see her, sometimes you don't. Now, tell me, how I can help? Advice is free. Chemicals and apparatus are available at a bargain price.' He smiled generously. 'I am known by all to be a helpful sort.'

Joe and Beth told him of their challenges. They shared their guesses about what might have caused Granelda's 'marble curse' and their ideas about Atticus and his purple drink. He sat back and listened patiently, though his fixed smile and un-seeable eyes made the Ravens uncomfortable. Beth wondered whether his expression changed a little when they mentioned the yellow poison and its possible remedy.

He bent towards them: 'Dear children, you have done *very* well. People will be *so* upset to hear about your Granelda. But I am at your service to help.'

Joe hit the science straightaway: 'Do you know what the yellow poison could be? And how it works?

I think it must precipitate a solid calcium compound from its organic—'

'...*calcium?*' interrupted a curious Dr McFudgett. Joe flipped a few brain cells to remember that calcium hadn't been discovered until a century later.

'Oh… er… it's a word I made up for things made of stone – like the statues.'

'I see.' Dr McFudgett brought his face and thick glasses to within inches of Joe's eyes and stared at him. Joe felt like sinking into the floor but stared back. The doctor breathed heavily but said nothing. Then he smiled again warmly and turned to Beth for her answer.

'We really want to find out who is attacking the Archers, and why,' she said. 'Maybe I shouldn't say so, but we think Lord Tresquin may have something to do with it.'

'Well… you are right again!' The doctor seemed pleased. 'He is deeply involved. It's all about the return of his twin brother. You have heard about the unfair archery match?'

'Yes, Sir,' said Joe energetically, 'and I discovered how the arrows were deflected – by magnets in the target and possibly magnetised arrow-heads.'

Dr McFudgett nodded and paused before he continued: 'I gather that after the contest, Lord Castus announced that he would come back to Caladrin when "Mars and Jupiter kissed". Ordinary people thought that was poetry, but it was a prediction from the stars. He loved astronomy as much as he loved archery and we both knew that in the year 1789 – *this year* – these two planets would overlap each other in the night sky.'

'A conjunction,' said Joe.

'Yes, Joe – you are right, *again*. Lord Castus chose this to be the sign of his return.' The doctor took a deep and noisy breath through his nose. 'Now… I've recently seen them moving towards each other, which means he will be back very soon!'

He paused to gauge Beth and Joe's reaction. Something inside told them to listen with interest but without saying anything. He carried on: 'At the archery contest, Lord Tresquin understood this plan, too, and he has been troubled ever since. He always wants me to let him know *exactly* when this conjunction will happen. He fears the return of Castus and the great rebellion he would bring with him. So he is "removing" all of his known supporters – the "Archers". Setting up their marble statues in public places was meant to scare them into giving up their ideas. But it hasn't worked.'

'How can we stop the poison being used?' asked Beth. 'We have already alerted all the Archers we know to avoid contact with anything yellow.'

'Have you really? How very clever!' said Dr McFudgett. 'And the purple drink?' he asked quickly. His face became serious.

'We have a sample here,' said Joe, pleased to show what they had collected. 'We want to know if it could be the answer to protecting the Archers, even bringing their statues back to life.'

'Where's it from?'

'Granelda's kitchen floor,' said Beth.

'I see. What great detectives you are! I'll place it on this table – the one with the distilling apparatus – and examine it later.'

As he did so, Joe heard the doctor say to himself, 'Careless boy!'

As the grandfather clock chimed, Dr McFudgett's smile returned in full width.

'I'm so sorry, that's all I have time to discuss today, my young friends. It seems I now have a special project to prepare this evening. I suggest you return to Mr Cringe – and Mr Haddock, of course – and come back tomorrow at teatime. I have had an idea that I know will interest you, and I can give you an answer about the purple liquid. Oh… Mr Cringe's son – Sacheverell? – do bring him along too. I would love to give you all an experience that will be unforgettable – one that will also solve all our problems at the same time!'

The Ravens offered thanks for the doctor's advice, then left. This time the same door took them out through the tradesmen's entrance, past a sickening smell of bad cabbages.

For a while, the Raven children walked in silence.

Beth spoke first: 'What did you think?'

'Wonderful scientist for his time,' said Joe. 'Interesting man with lots of ideas. But, do you know, I think his eyes might be different colours. Maybe *remonscrentium* got into him as a baby, too. Weird. Stay on high alert.'

'Please don't do anything silly.'

'No, great sister. How could I possibly upset our deputy mother, wise beyond her years.'

'Oh, shut up!'

'Are you bringing a swimming costume tomorrow?'

'No. It's your turn for a sinking feeling.'

'I've got one of those already.'

Next day, at Dodgison House the grand gate opened even before Joe pulled the bell. Sash was thrilled to be included in the outing to Dr McFudgett's. The idea of getting close to the Master of the Balloon gave him goose pimples. The doctor welcomed them each warmly, then led them through a locked door to reach his enormous yard.

'Here it is! The surprise of the afternoon!' he announced.

Jaws dropped and eyes widened. Before them was an enormous grey balloon, almost reaching to the top of the quarry. It was being filled through the system of barrels and pipes that Joe and Beth had spotted before. A large woven basket with round corners all in the same grey colour hung underneath.

'We are going for a ride!' The doctor seemed rounder than ever and in a particularly good mood. 'Come inside and I will explain.'

'Paradise! Perfect paradise!' was all Sash could utter as he walked in a daze back to the house. His head was already in the clouds.

In his small, book-filled study, Dr McFudgett served them a pink drink with brown biscuits. 'Nothing yellow, young friends,' he said with an easy smile. 'Now, let me tell you my plan: we agree that Lord Tresquin is making stone statues of the Archers to paralyse them before their hero, Lord Castus, returns to become the Duke. Yes?' They nodded. 'But before we can act, we must find first-hand proof of his plans. The Citadel is highly guarded, so we need a way of getting inside that is invisible and unexpected. How? We will travel to the rooftop, by balloon!'

'P-P-P-*amazing*!' Sash almost fainted with excitement.

'By pretending to be good friends with Lord Tresquin, I have learnt that he has a rooflight in the top corridor that he always leaves open. It's made for his pet eagle, but it's big enough for one of you to get through. I also know the layout of his private rooms. Because they are guarded so well from below, his study is never locked. So, Joe, would you be our frontline Citadel Explorer while the rest of us control the balloon? We'll hold it for your return, of course. Search his study for papers that would show his plan to destroy the Archers and ambush Lord Castus. It will be a dangerous mission – you never know what his bird will do. What do you think?'

'Yes, Sir,' said Joe, sitting up straight. 'Certainly.'

'But won't the balloon be seen by the guards long before we get there?' asked Beth.

'Pertinent,' mumbled Sash.

'Right, Beth! Well done. In truth, the risk is tiny. We have two special advantages: the first is the direction from which fly in. We'll be behind trees until the last minute. The second… well, you will see that when the balloon's grey covering is completely ready. It shouldn't take long before we can float away on our mission!'

'It's a hydrogen balloon, isn't it, Sir? A "*Charlière*"?' said Joe.

'As bright a young man as ever, Joe. Yes, it's the best! Not a "*Montgolfier*". That man and his brother are as full of hot air as his balloons, even if they can fly a sheep over Paris. No. Hydrogen will take you higher, for longer. No nasty fumes. No stoking a burner in mid-air. Can't catch fire – *much* safer.'

'But they can explode easily with an accidental spark, can't they, Sir?' asked Joe.

'*Theoretically*, of course…'

Beth thought that, for a moment, Dr McFudgett looked troubled, and that Joe could shut up being so clever.

'The weather this evening is fine and the wind *exactly* as I want it,' said the doctor. 'We won't be flying very high. It's an easy journey. Are we all signed up?'

The two boys gave a rousing chorus of 'Yes!' Beth nodded and managed a pale smile.

'Right! Good. We will be as safe as a mole in a molehill.'

'Dr McFudgett, Sir, may I ask if you found out what the purple liquid was made of?' asked Joe.

'Oh, just blueberry, onion and floor polish, I'm afraid. No exciting chemicals and none that could revive marble statues. A real pity, I know, but it was a good idea, Joe.

'Now, we have a short wait for the balloon to be completely ready, so let me show you around my most secret projects. There is just one I need to keep hidden for the moment, but you will have a chance to see how that works later.'

Beth, Joe and Sash followed him into building after building, all filled with different sorts of machines, glassware or strange creatures. They were still being dazzled by Dr McFudgett's inventions, when he looked at his watch and suddenly announced: 'Ready to go!'

The boys' excitement soared. Following the doctor towards the launch area, they pushed each other forward to get a good view. Beth walked slowly.

Everything was in place, except the balloon.

'Putrid periwinkles. It's gone!' cried Sash.

A light in their heads went out.

'Amazing, isn't it?' said Dr McFudgett, looking highly pleased. 'It's the grey paint, a new substance I've invented using chameleon skin. It makes the balloon and basket disappear into the background. It took me 354 chameleons to make that work.'

The boys were close to worshipping the doctor for such a brilliant idea. Beth wanted to hit him for killing so many beautiful animals.

'So, welcome to the first-ever chameleon-camouflaged balloon adventure! No matter where we go, we will not be seen. All aboard!' Dr McFudgett led the way – a cheerful Captain of the Flight.

Once in the basket, he recited the four key in-flight safety instructions: 'One: do not climb out of the basket. Two: do not crowd into any one space, causing basket imbalance. Three: do not throw anything out, including passengers. Four: do not vomit overboard when flying above a town.'

He then explained two important controls: 'This is the lever for take-off. A vacuum system – also my invention – holds the basket against the launching platform until I flip the lever to "RELEASE". Whatever you do, stay clear of it. We don't want you flying off on your own, do we?' he said with a broad smile. 'That would be dangerous.'

He grabbed a dangling piece of rope. 'This long cord is fixed to a flap at the top of the balloon. Pulling it down lets the hydrogen escape, and which makes the balloon descend.

'That's it! Simple! So… We are all… *set!*'

Sash shook with excitement.

Dr McFudgett jumped out of the basket, untied its four retaining ropes and climbed back in. 'Ready for the final mission? Then I'll—'

Rather than pull the vacuum lever for lift-off, he hit his head with his hand. 'I am… *stupid!* I've left the compass behind. Stay where you are for half a minute and I'll be back. Remember, don't touch a thing. We'll soon be off.'

He disappeared inside a nearby building where steam was belching out. The flying team waited. The doctor was taking a long time…

'I hope he hasn't lost it,' said Beth. 'I really want to get this mission over.'

'*Propulsion, please!*' said Sash.

Joe looked out of the basket. His stomach took a somersault. 'We're moving already!' he reported.

'What!' said Beth as she stared at the ground moving away.

'Perilous pimples!' said Sash, spinning his head round. 'We've left without the doctor!'

CHAPTER 14

ALL UP IN THE AIR

The invisible basket of Dr McFudgett's balloon carried its three perplexed passengers beyond the top of the trees.

'Did you touch the take-off lever, Joe?' said Beth. 'Look, it's in the "RELEASE" position! You—'

'No, I didn't. Honestly! It must have jumped there by itself. I don't think Sash did either. He was already airborne in his head.'

Joe looked over the side. Dr McFudgett had come out again and was waving gently. A sign to do something? But what? He looked oddly calm and smiled. A minute later he returned to the steam-shed and stayed there.

That was it.

The adventurers were on their own.

A stunned silence lasted only a few seconds before the dangers ahead trickled into their thoughts.

An angry Joe suddenly saw the point: 'He never intended to come with us. He must want us out of the way. All his friendliness was a show. What a—'

'...puffed-up, poisonous, putrid, pretender...' offered Sash.

The balloon flew beyond the top of the quarry. Here a stream of wind blew from the sea across the hills, pushing it towards the gardens of Boar Hall. They scanned the view all round. Their skin tingled. What could they do?

'Keep your eye on the horizon ahead, Mr Navigator,' called Joe.

'Yes, Sir!' responded Sash. 'Pupils polished and prepared!'

'Why don't we try to land on the grass? It's parkland and almost flat,' said Beth.

'I'd thought of that,' said Joe. 'Let's give the descent rope a try.' He pulled on the cord. It was stuck. He pulled harder. Its enormous length slithered into the basket.

The Ravens looked at each other.

'Before you ask, Beth, I *didn't* pull too hard... Let me have a look at it.'

He studied the rope with his Omniscope on its *Strong Close-up* setting. 'It was *meant* to come off,' he concluded. 'The top end has been cut nearly all the way through. Pulling it just snapped off the last few strands. What a great trick! Thanks, Doc!'

His mind filled with blackening thoughts. There was no way they could bring the balloon back to land.

'Crew – we're completely sabotaged,' Captain Joe announced.

'And we fell for it,' sighed Beth. 'For all he said, he's not on our side at all. He must be working for Lord Tresquin even though Mr Cringe thinks he's a great friend of the Archers.'

'No. He's got his own plans. Now he's milked us for what we know, dear Dr McTwoface can dispose of us. We must be in his way,' said Joe.

'And Sash?' asked Beth while their friend was looking out from the far side of the basket.

'Too close to us to be trusted.'

'What will happen?' said Beth, looking the colour of a mushroom.

'Well, fellow travellers, we'll go wherever the wind blows. We'll get higher and higher until the air gets thin. And we'll all get very cold. If we get into the stratosphere we'll get a bit warmer but run out of air pressure to keep us alive. And no one will see us because we are *"taking the first-ever chameleon-camouflaged balloon adventure".*'

No one spoke. Then: 'Plans, Captain?' asked Sash.

'We might have a sleep… play hide and seek… find somewhere to go fishing. We've got a nice long rope.'

'Joe, be *serious*! There's no way out of this, is there?' said Beth in a choked voice. 'If we stay climbing, we'll die of cold. If the balloon bursts before we run out of heat and air, we'll fall to our deaths.'

'Diagnosis correct!' His face twisted into several different shapes. 'I'm a bit short of plans at the moment, Sash. Perhaps we should look in the Weird Persons' *Guide* for Unlikely Survivors? It's in my pocket.'

He looked at Beth then put his finger to his lips and frowned. 'But please don't mention Thyr—'

A shout from Sash broke in: 'Hello! Navigator here! Peculiar finding! We're progressing the opposite way.'

Joe looked over the side. 'Check, Sash. Thanks. Different wind stream!' shouted Joe.

The rising balloon was flying back over the quarry, above Dr McFudgett's observatory and out to sea. Sash was speechless with delight at being so high. But for a moment, Joe and Beth became more interested in the scene below.

'Look!' said Joe. 'Two giant ships. Well-armed – fifty cannons I'd say – and small boats taking sailors to and from the beach.'

'Some are disappearing into a cave,' added Beth.

'Let's see what they are carrying.'

Joe's Omniscope came in handy again: 'Boxes, barrels – and guns.'

When he looked over the edge of the basket to get a better view a shrill whistle blasted out.

'Piercing pain!' complained Sash with his hands over his ears.'

'Sorry, Sash. It won't last long,' said Joe. 'We must have static electricity on board!'

He looked along the inside of the basket: it was clear. He looked over the edge: nothing suspicious.

'Camouflaged?' said Beth quietly. 'You may have to *feel* for it…'

'Hmm.'

At the risk of hitting kilovolts of static electricity or falling into the sea, Joe leant far out to feel along the outside. Yes. Something was there. He fingered its shape. A box had been fixed to the side and he knew at once what it contained: a Leyden jar – or perhaps several. Joe's EAR reached peak volume. He switched it off to save Sash from a meltdown.

His fingers also found two wires running from the box in different directions. Each of them ran to a different corner of the basket where they turned up to follow a supporting rope towards the balloon. In the evening light, his face went as white as chalk.

'Well, thanks to Dr Frankenstein we have another choice of how we die – by explosion. He has fixed a powerful spark to ignite the hydrogen.'

'Can you tell when?' asked Beth.

'I don't know. A quarter past one, perhaps? It's a popular time on this outing.'

'*Please* take this seriously! We are heading for death, Joe – and taking Sash with us. I'm sorry, but I'm going to call on Thyripolis for help. You've got all sorts of knowledge and gadgets, and you've worked out what's happening *so* well. And you're really kind. I know you think the silver bird is just an ornament and only comes to life in my head, but I really wish you could see him in action. Maybe you can't. Perhaps you don't want to. I don't know.

We have to go with what we each believe in – and I believe he's *amazing*.'

'OK, Beth. Sorry. I just can't fit him into how I know the universe works. I keep my feet on solid ground... Well, not at the moment – they're miles up in the air!'

'Maybe we do need a bird?' said Beth, half smiling.

They both sighed, then: 'Over to the young lady in flight,' Joe said cheerfully. 'You can drive. I'll stay working for a solution I can understand.'

Beth nodded.

'I'm going to hop over the side,' said Joe. 'There'll either be a timing mechanism in the box or a pressure monitor that will fire the spark. I'll see if I can disable either of those or else release the Leyden jar into the sea.'

'You mustn't get out of the basket, Joe. Remember the rule.'

Joe snorted. 'Dr McFalsehood doesn't bother with rules. And I'm not planning to disappear in the next Big Bang. Can you get Navigator Sash to bring over the rope? You'll have to take his hands off his ears first.'

At Joe's direction, Sash and Beth wound the rope round his waist several times then held on to an end each. He collected tools from his OAK, sat on the edge of the basket and looked out. The ships below looked so small now.

'Crew, I'm going let myself down outside the basket near the box. I'll hang on to the side while I go then I'll need both hands free. That's when you'll need to take my full weight on the rope. All right?'

'Perfectly perceived,' said Sash, looking petrified.

Beth nodded again. Words weren't easy, but she managed some practical advice: 'In case the rope slips, how about tying it to the metal pipe that supports the RELEASE lever?'

'Safety ahoy! Will do!'

When everything was in place, Joe clambered over the side. He made an awkward 180-degree turn and let himself down, holding on to the edge as long as he could.

'Take!' he shouted.

'Right!' confirmed Beth and Sash.

Joe let go and slid down and stopped with a jolt. His weight took the crew by surprise. They were pulled sharply forward, losing their balance, but were caught by the side of the basket. It dented with a creak as they hit it. They held on hard enough not to lose the rope, but Joe fell further down than he had planned.

'Pull me up a bit!' he shouted.

'Right!'

Tugging hard worked, but the basket cracked and bent where it was supporting the rope.

'Work quickly, Joe,' Beth shouted. 'The basket's beginning to collapse.'

'I am! But there's no easy way into the box. It's completely sealed and I can't see how it's fixed. I'll use my DAD to see if there's any sound inside.'

With his wind-chilled hands and an aching back he extracted his Digital Audio Detector, pressed two buttons and pushed it against the box. In a few seconds it relayed a ticking noise and a small screen reported 'Probable timepiece'.

'Got it! I'm coming back,' he shouted. 'Can you pull me up again? I can't reach the edge.'

They pulled as hard as they could. Joe began to move higher until, under the pressure of the rope, the side of the basket collapsed completely. Joe plummeted down again. Sash and Beth tried to hold on, but Joe's fall was too sudden and too strong. They had to let go before they fell out. He jolted down further – until the RELEASE pipe took up the slack, and held.

His recovery from there needed good teamwork. Joe, with weakening fingers, gripped the rope and inched upward by hand. Beth and Sash each hauled on their end of the rope to shorten his journey. When reached the basket, there was no ledge to hang on to. Getting him inside was a desperate struggle in which all three adventurers came close to tumbling overboard. With a last surge of his aching arms, he made it. Scraping his legs on the broken edge, he finally flopped with the others onto the floor. The RELEASE pipe, bent right over, was half torn away from its anchor.

'Thanks for the anti-gravity muscles, team,' said Joe when he had found his breath. 'My detector says there's a clock mechanism in the box for triggering the explosion. So we're all still at risk.'

'Persistently puzzling, perhaps predicting that we'll perish prematurely but permanently?' said Sash.

'You've got the idea,' said Joe. 'Perfectly.'

'What's Plan P?' said Sash. 'Erm – I mean Plan B…'

'B is for… Bolts. The box might be fixed on by nuts and bolts, but I can't see any…' Beth cleared her throat.

'I know – it's the camouflage again,' continued Joe.

The chief navigator took a close interest in the broken section of the basket. 'Puzzling potatoes! There's broken wire sticking out,' said Sash.

All-ears, Joe leapt up to look. 'Great find!' he said, giving Sash an encouraging slap on the back, then quickly grabbing his arm to stop him toppling into the sea. 'We've accidentally broken the fatal circuit. The broken wire will stop the charge reaching the top of the balloon. Risk now declared low!'

In spite of this, Joe decided it best to put the high electric charge permanently out of the way. He felt his way to four fixing nuts on the inside of the basket and, with a tool from his kit, worked to remove them. As he pushed at the last bolt, the box fell from the side of the basket. Everyone watched it fall. A short way down, it stopped, suspended from the basket by its other wire.

'Right!' said Joe. 'The final parting…' He conjured up a short, laser-edge beam to cut it through. 'Here goes…'

As it fell, the metal-coated jar glinted in the low setting sun. When it hit the sea, it triggered a violent bright light followed by a sharp cracking sound. The flying crew's fists flew into the air with a cry of, 'Yes!' All went quiet.

'We're still going up,' said Sash.

'I'm thinking about it,' said Joe.

Beth was crouched in a corner, her head buried in her hands and her breathing deep.

'Maybe I could climb up outside the balloon and make a few holes,' said Joe.

'Perchance you would precipitate yourself into a perpendicular plunge,' said Sash.

'Maybe I'll die anyway... Maybe we'll all die anyway.'

As the sun disappeared, Joe's mood darkened. Short of any ideas, exhausted and still floating higher out to sea, everyone's hope for survival had all but gone. With the air getting thinner and colder, their drowsiness drifted slowly into sleep. Joe doubted that he would ever wake up again. The balloon continued to climb.

Much later, Beth's eyes blinked and opened. Her vision was blurred. She was achingly cold all over. Was it morning? A growing silvery mist swirled round; a strange light shone from above. A now-familiar feeling crept over her. She could never describe the sense of a tingly skin and being wrapped in warm air that she felt when Thyripolis was near.

The boys were still lying like lumps, close to the edge of the damaged basket. She uncurled herself slowly and looked out. Through the mist, what she saw made her check that she really was awake. Not only were they flying much lower but they were also heading towards the coast.

'Land ahoy!' she shouted to the crew. 'Wake up!'

Sash woke quickly and saw what was happening. 'A

prominent protuberant popping of my pupils!' he said. 'How did we do that?'

'A different wind…' said Beth.'A very different wind altogether.'

Joe, still asleep, tried to turn off his alarm.

'Panic over!' shouted Sash into his ear.

Joe jumped up and saw how low they were flying. He heard himself say, 'Good navigation, Sash!' but clashing thoughts fought in his head over how that could possibly have happened: *Unusual weather – unlikely; a tear in the balloon letting the hydrogen out? That might be too fast. It can't be done – it has been done. We might not die in flight after all – we could still die landing.* The thought that Beth and her Thy-bird played a part was surprisingly hard to push away. But… a better idea… the camouflage paint had caused the balloon material to leak hydrogen at an ideal rate and the wind was favourable. Possibly.

'Passing the physician's periscope,' reported Sash, indicating the doctor's observatory.

'Look! There's light coming out of his lift shaft,' said Beth.

'I *can* see it, Beth,' said Joe in a grumpy voice.

'I wonder if *he* might see *us?*' she said.

'Who cares? We're camouflaged anyway – remember?'

The crew stared ahead as the balloon drifted slowly towards Caladrin. Beth noticed a change in the light and that the mist was fading. She guessed that Thyripolis was moving. What she did not see was that he had soared up in a big circle, then, on his way down, split into three separate birds heading towards them.

Everyone watched the ground rushing into view as the balloon fell rapidly out of the air.

'Poltergeists! We're plunging!' shrieked Sash.

'Going down,' announced Joe. 'Ground floor: garden-ware, gnomes, special offers. And the way out!' Joe's thoughts had fired up in relief at the chance of landing safely.

The balloon was not only descending fast but also changing direction. Working together, the three forms of the silver bird were steering it across the lake at Boar Hall. When the travellers were nearly at the far side, close to a small ancient dwelling, Joe made a further announcement: 'Correction: basement level: fishing bait, swimsuits, snorkels.'

They braced themselves against the good side of the basket as the surface of the lake flashed past them inches below. Then, in an eruption of water, stones and earth they landed, half in the lake and half on the shore.

'Wha— ah...' Sash's voice rang out as he fell through the broken basket-side into the water. Joe and Beth were ejected with a thump onto nearly dry ground. Everything stopped. An owl hooted. Sash tried to navigate his way back to the shore. As soon as she could, Beth grabbed the rope and threw him one end.

'P-p-perishing! But p-p-perfect!' was all he could say as he shivered his way inland.

Sitting on a large stone, they huddled together under a tree.

'Peculiar, isn't it?' said Sash, as they watched a strange disturbance of the moon-lit lake where the just visible balloon was sinking.

A short creaking sound made them look round sharply. Somewhere a door was opening. Should they run, or hide? The snap of a nearby twig made them squeeze together even harder. A dark-robed figure, slightly bent, was walking towards them carrying a candle. His face, if he had one, was hidden within an enormous hood. Their eyes held him in a fixed stare as he came towards them.

CHAPTER 15

THE HOODED MAN

From the depths of his hood, the man spoke: 'Don't be afraid, children.'

The voice was close to a whisper but so calm that the three adventurers at once felt safer.

'I have been expecting you, though I wasn't told you would arrive from the sky! Come into my small house. It's warm, and I do have a few refreshments.'

At this invitation, the children's fears melted. They followed him in silence to his angled stone dwelling where the heat of an open wood fire curled round them. An oil lamp added to its light but cast menacing shadows on the walls. A tall bookcase, a chair and an old table were his only furniture.

Sash began steaming, and his eyes closed with relief.

The man spoke again: 'I believe you are Beth, Joe, and' – here the man swallowed hard – 'Sa... Sacheverell... aren't you?'

'Yes, Sir,' said Beth and Joe. Sash was too smothered in warmth to reply.

The hooded man offered hot drinks – thin, rich broth that took away their hunger as well as their thirst. He invited them to sit on the floor, on a rush mat. He found an old blanket to cover them, then sat on the floor himself.

'Dear, brave children, we are fighting for the same thing. As a hermit, I am helping Lord Castus to return. I know that the Archers have long been expecting him to claim his true inheritance, but now his return is near, they are made to suffer more than ever. You have seen their statues?'

Everyone nodded quietly as gruesome images of the poisoned families flooded their thoughts.

'Mr Cringe has told me about your wonderful work in discovering the poison that is destroying them. Well done! What a great step forward! Lord Castus so hates this suffering and wants it to stop, but the forces against him coming back are the most cunning and powerful in the world. The people of this land are being deceived and they don't know who to trust.'

'Like the Doctor of Dodgison House?' said Joe.

'Yes, like Dr McFudgett.'

The hermit's mind seemed to drift for a moment, then he took down two books and put them in a small pile on the table. 'Something sweet for you?' He opened the top book, took out a round sponge cake full of jam and cut it into four pieces. 'Hermits aren't allowed to eat these... Do have a piece.' Everyone ate one slice and he returned the empty 'books' to the shelf.

'How can we find the *antidote* to the yellow poison?' asked Beth. 'We're sure it's purple. We found a riddle we think means we have to go underwater to find it.'

'Have you been under any water yet?' the hermit asked.

'Yes! Particularly penetrating water, perchance,' said a thawing Sash. 'I'm still permeated if not polluted.'

'There's nothing to find in the lake, Sacheverell. I wish there was,' he said. 'I know it well.'

'So, logically, we should explore the river or the sea,' said Joe. 'Let's take a step back.'

'No room,' said Sash.

'No, not with our legs, Sash – in our *thinking*. What do we know already? The poison is yellow, and Atticus relies on Mr Haddock to keep his supplies coming. Mr Haddock works in your Manufactory, *near the river*.'

'Mr Haddock?' said Sash. His face turned bright red in spite of the cold. 'Preposterous! A pernicious possibility – patently poppycock. He is the purest person on the planet.'

'Suppose he doesn't *know* he's helping the enemy,' offered Beth. 'Perhaps he's just sending something yellow for a customer's experiments that then gets made into the poison.'

'Like the yellow frogs?' said Sash.

'Yes! That's it! The yellow frogs!' said Joe. 'Sending

them to the clever doctor. But if so, the clever doctor must also have the antidote. It would be too risky to handle the poison without it.'

'Atticus did say that the antidote came to him by a different route,' said Beth. 'But Dr McFudgett doesn't live by the river or the sea.'

'If he doesn't *make* it at Dodgison House, he must *store* it there – probably in one of his outbuildings,' said Joe. 'Maybe it has to be kept in water?'

The hidden voice spoke again: 'So you will need to start your search there. And you will need to start now. There is very little time left.'

The hermit's words took a somersault in the air before hitting Joe's *Start* button. 'Then let's go, crew!' he said. 'This is what we came for.'

Joe could never work out why at this point he looked up. He stared at the top of the bookcase. The name 'Thyripolis' escaped his lips in a whisper. The silver bird was sitting still, visible in the firelight but also with a glow of its own.

'He is my constant companion, Joe,' said the hermit. Beth's heart jumped and Sash looked up too, but they said nothing.

'Oh,' said Joe flatly. '…Interesting. Granelda had one of those…'

A soft comment by the hermit relieved Joe from feeling awkward: 'Yes, she's a wise and thoughtful lady.'

'I've an idea,' said Beth, on task, 'a way we might get into Dr McFudgett's outbuildings. *We use his lift shaft.* Remember when we flew over the coast, we saw a light there and sailors unloading barrels into a cave? If Dr McFudgett can reach the lift from his outbuildings and the sailors can get to the bottom of the shaft, there must be a complete tunnel between him and the sea.'

Joe wished he didn't feel so cross when Beth had bright ideas, and the image of the silver bird had not yet faded away. He stayed quiet.

'Perspicacious!' said Sash. 'That would put the pernicious physician in closer proximity to the sea than predicted!'

'Beth, that is inspired. I would be glad to help as much as I can,' said the hermit. 'The lift shaft does give us our greatest hope.' He looked out of his door. 'The moon has clouded over, but we can't wait. Deep darkness will help our cover, but it will also make our journey difficult. Still, I know this landscape well and I can lead you to the observatory by a little-known path.'

'Thank you!' said Joe. 'I'll get Dr McMischief's long rope.'

It was a long, dark trek uphill, though the moon sometimes spilt its cold light in patches along the way. Climbing over rocks, squeezing under low branches and jumping across small streams took them to the hill-top observatory. As soon as they reached the lift shaft, Joe, the smallest of the group, volunteered to 'go below', leaving the others as base-camp support. He climbed the few stone steps over the circular wall and lowered himself into the shaft. Then he used a focused daylight beam from his PEST to identify the metal catch he was looking for. Though rusty, its handle turned with a squeak. A platform from the bottom of the shaft flew up to just below his feet.

'Boarding for descent!' he shouted, jumping on. It hardly moved. 'Weight!'

'I *am* waiting,' said Beth.

'No, I need more *weight*. The counterbalance is made for Dr McBulbous. I need to be heavier.'

The team gathered stones and Joe added them to the platform until it moved down a little. 'One more small stone… and… we're off!'

Holding one end of the long rope, his travel downwards through the darkness was easy. At the bottom, using a dim light from his PEST, he fastened the lower platform catch and stepped on to a stone floor. As arranged, he gave the rope two quick pulls to let the team know he was there, then tied it to a nearby rafter.

The smell of the sea stung his nose. He was definitely in a tunnel from the beach. With a PEST-powered navigation beam, he moved out of the lift area to find a path running beside a long channel of water. He shivered. What was the chance of McFudgett being down here even at night? Were the sailors all back in their galleons? Ears and eyes at full sensitivity reported no signs of life except for a rat scrabbling along the floor.

Which way to go? For the distance he could see, the view was the same in both directions: a channel with a path alongside.

'Ooh!' A spot of icy water dropped heavily on his head from the rock above. He looked up, but his PEST light beam revealed nothing except round patches of damp. Another drop fell on his face. A memory pushed itself into his mind of when the *Guide* showed the watery riddle that brought him here. *Is this another 'message'?* He took out the book, but it did nothing. Out of curiosity, he opened it one page further on. There was a new picture: a compass – no writing, just a grey circle with a spinning black needle in the centre. He held the book flat. The needle pointed in the direction of the water channel to his left. 'Are you telling me that's north – the way I need to go?' he enquired. *Did I really just speak to a dumb book?* The *Guide* gave no answer.

'Well, it's the only hint we have,' he said, thinking out loud. 'Let's try it.' On his first step forward, the grey circle turned green. Joe stopped. 'Promising – and the other way?' He stepped in the opposite direction and, though the needle stayed where it was, the circle glowed red. 'The right way and the wrong way,' said Joe. 'That's the closest to a "guide" this book's ever been. OK… Lead on.' *Did I talk to it again?*

His walk was painfully quiet except for his footsteps, interrupted by an occasional 'splip' of water falling from the roof. After the balloon episode, his limbs were stiff. Now, at the fear of being discovered, their tightness was growing. He quickened his pace and made good headway until he heard them: distant voices calling to one another. Then the splashing of oars echoing off the rock of the long tunnel. Joe's intense hope that the sailors were staying on the beach was dashed. He switched off his PEST, stretched out flat on the path and leant low by the water to look towards them. In the distance he saw two men in a long, thin boat. One was rowing. The other stood towards the back, holding a weak light with one hand and resting the other on what Joe guessed to be a long barrel lying on its side. They were still positioned between the sea and the shaft. There was nowhere to for him to hide and he would soon be seen, either if he ran back or ran onward towards McFudgett's estate. They had to be stopped…

His first thought was to sink the boat, but the PEST's infrared laser was too weak to burn a hole in it at that distance, especially if he had to beam it through the water to keep himself out of view. A piece of sailor would be a better target at first. Staying flat, he pulled out his Omniscope and set it to *Thermal Imaging*. Two more adjustments were needed: to add a cross-wire to identify the chosen target and a microwave link to his PEST to fine-tune the angle of its beam. Using a low-power infrared laser, he pin-pointed the sailor's hand that held the light. His quiet command, '*Link and fire*,' caused just the right effect: the sailor shrieked and pulled his hand away sharply. The lamp fell into the water and went out. The other sailor stopped rowing to help his shipmate.

In the deep darkness of the tunnel Joe scrambled to his feet and ran towards the sea just beyond the shaft, where the path ended. From the sound of splashing and the sailors' voices he judged himself now close enough to fire his invisible hot laser at full power without being seen. The beam did its job. His Omniscope confirmed a clear hit on the boat below the waterline. The sailors sank rapidly.

Joe returned at speed, as planned, towards his appointment at the doctor's. The *Guide* kept a constant bearing until the path stopped suddenly at a stone wall. Close by was a small jetty and behind it, an enormous door. *The route of the devilish doctor's deliveries*, diagnosed Joe.

At the wall, the water in the channel turned to the right, flowing under a stone arch into a cavern. Was he imagining that the water there was glowing? He looked again at the compass. The needle had moved, pointing to the cavern. He took a small pace backwards – it went red; forward again – it turned green. *Really? Go forward?* There was no way across but to swim… The 'sinking' fell to Joe. He folded his coat and left it on the jetty with the *Guide*. Stuffing his complete waterproof OAK in the pocket of his breeches, he jumped in. The water was screamingly cold. His white and blue body shrieked to get out, but, on override, his brain allowed no other choice but straight on. *This is the only way to change history, remember?*

He swam in near darkness under the arch into a large, round, underground pool. Relief! It was much warmer than the channel. The pool also had a landing stage, close to another door. A small boat with oars was tied up to it. On the stage itself, several barrels lay on their side. From one trickled a jelly-like sludge surrounded by a dark liquid. Joe tried to swim towards it, but a strong underwater current pulled him the other way. He was drawn through a curtain of green fronds towards the centre of the pool. As he was dragged below the surface, the purple glow grew brighter. Sinking deeper, he bumped into its underwater source: a fantastic seahorse, half his height. Purple light was spreading out from a large pouch in its transparent body. While he looked, more seahorses crowded round, all floating calmly, crinkly heads above curled tails. *These are the source of the antidote!*

Joe strained his way to the nearby jetty, but as he clambered out of the water he slipped on spilt jelly. It was the remains of a seahorse. While the water drained off his clothes, he stared between the jelly and the majestic creatures moving towards him. His eyes watered as he looked at the seahorses directly. 'You are amazing! Beautiful! I don't usually say, "beautiful", but you are.' He shook his head. 'I'm *so* sorry. Dr McFilthy has brought you here from the sea, not because you're amazing creatures but because your purple insides give him power.' While speaking, he was aware that, as they collected around him, the purple lights of the seahorses became brighter. He sighed again, deeply. 'Sorry, must go, lads! Hide where you can! We're all trying to get out of here alive.'

Joe tried the nearby door. It, too, was locked – but he had to see what lay behind. He could laser-cut the lock, but the risk of setting fire to the surrounding wood was too high. So he went for the old trick of locksmiths and robbers. Retrieving his OAK quickly, he took a steel rod to the door. Threading it through the keyhole, he pushed out the heavy key inside. It fell with a satisfying clang on the stone floor beyond. With his neodymium magnet and the rod, he connected with the key and pulled it underneath the door. Success! The door creaked open.

Joe crept into darkness filled with a sickening smell like rotting fish. He triggered his PEST to give a dim downward light. Around him was a stone hallway with a side room. In these were barrels full of dead seahorses, emptied of their purple liquid. Other barrels were filled with frog parts without their skins. Joe guessed that these remains were to be dumped at sea after their owners had been killed to serve Dr McFudgett's plans.

He pushed into a large room ahead – as round as any other in Dr McFudgett's domain. Surely this was the headquarters of his secret manufactory. Joe risked lighting an oil lamp on a table and looked round. Workbenches were laid out along two sides, all holding strange-shaped flasks, crushers, knives, suckers, bottles, filters and pipettes. One side was set up to make the powdered poison. The shelves there carried rows of flasks filled with a murky yellow oil. Other bottled ingredients included 'Small Whale-Juice', 'Extract of Worm Intestine', 'Pig's Eye Vitreous' and 'Crushed Maggot'. On the purple side, there was a mass of onions and lemons, and a few berries. Bottles of purple '*Raw SH Digestant*' were lined up for processing.

Beyond the workbenches, shelves on both sides, from floor to ceiling, supported jars of the finished potions. Joe looked at the notices beside them. The ingredients of the poison, *'Powder of Coagulosolidum'*, was listed with instructions for turning it into different forms of 'treatment'. On the opposite side, jars of the antidote, *'Salvium'*, were labelled either *'Protective Strength'* or – could Joe believe his eyes? – *'Corrective Strength'*.

'That's it!' he said in a loud whisper. 'A corrective potion! We can return our poisoned Archers to normal.' He took a jar from the shelf and held it closely. 'Yes!' He imagined a restored Granelda with all the Archers breaking out of their stone prisons and having a party. 'But how do we use it? They can't drink it or breathe it… Pour it on them?' He pulled a face. 'We need a spray. Maybe there's one here. Dr McWormface must have given one to Atticus.' He began a search in a long line of cupboards. Yes! The third one contained a shelf-full. His thoughts returned to a happy ending. All that was left to do was take the *Salvium* and lots of spray guns to the Archers and—

A flapping noise above made him look up. Risking an encounter with the doctor, he directed his PEST towards it. There was nothing to see except a feather floating down slowly. Not a usual feather, though. It shone as though it were made of fine silver filaments. He followed it with his eyes until it landed on a table, then moved closer. It began to evaporate into a silver mist. As it disappeared, he struggled hard to agree with himself that this must be from Beth's bird. When the mist had disappeared, he re-focused his logical eyes on the piece of paper where the feather had landed. It was headed *'Stonemasons' Targets'*. As Joe stared at the names, he felt sick, then wild with anger at McFudgett's scheme. All the people he knew were there: Granelda, Mr Pinwell, Mr Cringe, their families – and many more. One particular name grabbed his brain by the synapses: *Lord Tresquin*. He stared at it, making sure he had read it correctly. 'That proves it,' he said quietly. 'McFudgett is working not for the Duke, nor for the Archers… *nobody*. All of this is *his* plan – for *his* power.'

He put the paper in his pocket, and as fast as he could, loaded the boat with all the sprays and as many jars of *Salvium-CS* as he could without it sinking. He rowed back to the lift shaft, tied up the boat and pulled the rope three times.

A voice echoed down from above. 'We can hear you if you shout!'

'I've got bottles of the antidote! It's from seahorses! I'll have to put them on McFudgett's platform to bring them up.'

'The seahorses?'

'No, jars of the strong purple stuff.'

Together, using the pulley system, Beth and Sash helped him to lift out the first load. Sash was lowered down to help move the goods more quickly. It took four more boat trips to collect all they could.

When their mission was finished, everyone sat near the top of the shaft catching a brief rest. Watching the sky get lighter, Joe talked about what he had found. He showed everyone the list of the Stonemasons' targets.

The hermit spoke as calmly as usual: 'So, you have found out that the doctor, "helpful to all", is really using

– destroying – everyone for his own ends. Evil is so easily hidden behind smiles, though it will always show itself in the end.'

'What do we do?' asked Beth.

'We can't stay here for long. Anyway, we need to use the antidote as soon as possible,' said the hermit.

'Can we take some to Granelda?' asked Beth. 'If she is not yet completely marbled she might be able to drink it.' Joe gave an enthusiastic thumbs-up for that, and the hermit agreed. 'We could use the spray on Merrin as well,' she added.

Joe's thumbs wilted without his noticing.

'Here's an idea,' said the hermit. 'For speed, we can hide most of our catch – Joe's catch – in the hollow near my house. If we cover it with fallen branches, no one will find it. In daylight Sacheverell and I can use a covered horse and cart to take everything to the Manufactory. Joe and Beth can take a spray and the antidote to Quince Cottages. What do you think?'

All agreed.

The hermit stood up slowly and took a deep breath. 'Good young people, we are nearly at the end of our quest. So, thank you. I know that Lord Castus will be more than pleased with what you have done for him. There is time now for a brief sleep and breakfast before we set out on a rather different journey. We pray that the morning sun will bring light to replace our darkness – but there are still challenges to face. Our rescue still has unseen hazards.'

CHAPTER 16

CLOCKING A SUCCESS

Joe and Beth had already filled the spray apparatus with *Salvium* before they hurried to Quince Cottages. Joe looked in the window. Granelda was laid back in her chair, completely white, rigid and with her eyes closed. Was she breathing? He couldn't tell.

Inside the house, the air was cold and damp. They passed quickly through to the sitting room, where the sight of Granelda churned them up with anger and sadness.

'Hello, Granelda!' called Beth, trying to sound cheerful. There was no response.

'You may have to speak louder,' said Joe. 'The nerves in her ears and brain won't be working properly.'

Beth moved closer. '*Granelda!*'

The old lady's eyes opened very slowly, misty-white and staring. Her face showed exhausted anger, of having given up the fight. Joe stepped forward and spoke clearly, louder than usual: 'We need to give you this, Granelda.' He showed her the jar of purple liquid.

'Joe, you'll make her even more worried doing that! She saw it last when the imposters were here. If we ask her to drink it she might think we're on *their* side.'

'Oh… Sorry.'

'Why don't we put some drops in her eyes and ears? You've still got your pipette, haven't you?'

'Yes.'

Explaining what they were doing, they carefully administered the purple *Salvium* – and waited.

No change.

'It won't work instantly – even the Corrective Strength will take time to seep in,' said Joe.

'Yes, I know. But I thought it might work fast enough for us to see *some* result.'

'Let's use the spray,' said Joe. 'Her eyes have closed again, so it won't upset her. She'll be numb all over anyway. We could squirt some into her mouth, too.'

The treatment was given as Joe suggested, though they had no idea of how much to use. After this, they could think of nothing else to do. They looked intensely at her face, willing her to wake up – but there was no change. Beth spotted Thyripolis, the ornament, on the mantelpiece. He was completely still, though his eyes followed her every movement. Her heart jumped and her internal voice cried out for his help again. Joe hadn't noticed and was eager to go.

When they were halfway down the path, Beth remembered: 'We've forgotten Merrin!'

'Oh, bother Merrin! Her tongue's more spikey than a porcupine,' said Joe. 'We'll get round to her later.'

'But she's spikey because she's been poisoned, remember? We've not seen the real Merrin. If the antidote works, she'll be her old cheerful self.'

Joe paused. 'OK. Give her a spray – there's some left. I'll start walking back to the Boarham jetty and you can catch me up.'

As he opened the gate, a wiff arrived. Checking that the road was empty, he took a note from its hairy pouch. The envelope was addressed to him and to Beth. It read:

To the Archers and valued helpers,
Come as quickly as you can to the Manufactory.
We need to prepare. Bring what you can.
Things are moving faster than expected.
Jarek Cringe

Prepare? For what? thought Joe. He ran back to tell Beth and met her leaving the house.

'I can't find Merrin!' said Beth. 'It must be Chelkwyn's work. Horrid, horrid man!'

'We've got to get back to Jarek fast,' said Joe. 'Something's happening and he'll need the *Salvium*. Come on!'

They ran out of the gate, along the road and into Shepherd's Way.

THUMP!

They collided with a short, solid man heading towards them. Beth dropped the spray apparatus and a purple puddle began to spread round his feet.

'We're *really* sorry, Sir,' said Beth.

'Stupid idiots! I should think so! You should look where you're going rather than charge about as though nobody else existed. Weren't you ever taught that children are to *walk* when out, not run?'

'I'm *so* sorry, Sir,' said Joe. 'I hope we haven't splashed your shoes.'

The man looked down and took a sharp breath in. 'What... is... *that?*'

In the awkward pause while Joe raced to think of a suitable answer, the man's expression changed from angry red to pale fury. His eyes narrowed. 'Let me pick it up for you,' he said in a clipped voice, trying to sound ordinary. Keeping hold of the spray apparatus, he continued: 'This is... *unusual*. Where did you get it, boy?'

Joe couldn't think quickly enough to find an explanation other than: 'We're friends of Dr McFudgett.' *How could I say that?* 'He knows I've loved inventing things since I was very small. He thought I might like to try it out' – a bright idea popped into his mind – 'before delivering it to Mr Chelkwyn.'

'We believe he lives not far from here,' said Beth.

The man looked very hard at them both, then stared into Joe's eyes. 'Is that so? Well, you have reached the right person. I am Mr Chelkwyn.'

Powered by a brain working overtime, Joe immediately smiled and looked delighted. 'How very helpful, Sir! Thank you. That saves us a longer journey and means we can give you something else that's been newly invented by the doctor.'

'Which is…?'

Joe retrieved his OAK and brought out the 'gift'. 'It's a Pan-Electromagnetic Spectrum Torch. You may not have come across one of those, but Dr McFudgett says it will soon become brilliant. I'll show you.'

Mr Chelkwyn's anger disappeared. He had been favoured with a gift from the amazing Doctor.

'If you look into here' – he held the torch up to Mr Chelkwyn's eye – 'I'll show you how it works.' Joe clicked on the device.

Mr Chelkwyn jumped backward with loud cry and flung a hand over his eye. 'What was *that?*' he cried. 'Give me it now!'

'Oh! I'm *so* sorry, Sir! It must have been set in the wrong mode. Oh, dear! Let me try a different setting on the other eye.'

'*No!* No! Keep away!'

'It will be *fine*, really. It won't hurt this time. I've reset it. Dr McFudgett showed me how.'

'Hold my hand for a moment,' offered Beth to Mr Chelkwyn in a soothing voice. 'That might help.'

Indeed, it did help – it left Joe unhindered to apply his intense white beam to the second eye. With another shout of pain, and covering both eyes with his hands, Mr Chelkwyn leant against the wall for support.

'Oh, no!' said Joe. 'Maybe Dr McFudgett isn't quite the man he makes himself out to be. But don't worry, Sir. This will just make you look at the future differently. You could try some yellow eye drops at home.' Mr Chelkwyn, still blinded, groped for a few steps along the wall, then sank to the ground.

'Sorry, we do have to go now,' said Beth as she picked up the spray.

They hurried towards the landing stage near Boar Hall. 'We caught Mr Chelkwyn just in time,' she said. 'He was on his way to take Granelda away.'

With a shout of, 'Alfonce!', Beth was able to summon the boatman to deliver them to the Manufactory.

He was unusually excited and full of words: 'I really dunno what's going on. The river's gone mad!' he said. 'Yesterday, dozens of the Duke's private army were shipped from Caladrin to the Fortress. A strange trading vessel came into the harbour early. Unloaded dozens of strong boxes. Some went to Caladrin. Some went to our landing stage. Then it dropped a wide dinghy – white and gold with a blue canopy in front. Yer don't see those often. The foreign ship had gone by morning.'

'Was it—' tried Joe, but with no impact on Alfonce's avalanche of words.

'There are rumours, of course. Some say Lord Castus is about to return. That would do us very well – we've all had enough of Tresquin. Not that he's shown his head for days.'

'What are *you* going to do?' asked Beth.

'Me? Keep my ferry service going, as always. Trade should pick up with all these goings-on. Otherwise, stay quiet.'

At the Manufactory, Sash and the hermit were already outside, unloading the cart.

'Princely punctuality,' said Sash. 'Plans prosecuted with perfection?'

'We used the antidote on Granelda, though nothing changed while we were there,' said Beth. 'Merrin had been taken away.'

'And we've removed Mr Chelkwyn from Dr McFudgett's service,' said Joe.

'You have done well,' said the hermit. 'I will find Mr Cringe in the Manufactory.'

'I'll go, Sir,' said Sash. 'I can predict where he's presently present.'

'Thank you, Sacheverell.'

As Sash walked to the main entrance, the hermit watched him closely all the way.

Mr Cringe and Sash re-appeared quickly. What surprised the adventurers was that, on meeting, Mr Cringe and the hermit gave each other a hug, leaving Sash to join his friends.

'Peculiar!' said Sash. 'I've never perceived my father do that to anyone previously.'

Beth wondered if Sash would like to have added, …*not even me.*

Mr Cringe and the hermit, smiling and calm, joined the young crew.

'Joe, tell Mr Cringe what we found,' said the still-hooded voice.

Joe couldn't wait: 'We've found the purple liquid that restores people who've been poisoned!'

'You're telling us you have an antidote – a *curative* antidote?' said Mr Cringe.

The explorers nodded. 'We've got a huge pile of bottles of it—' said Joe.

'And we've got spray guns to make it work fast—' added Beth.

'...by the pressurised propulsion of a purple potion towards our petrified population,' said Sash.

Mr Cringe's whole body expanded. His face lit up. 'Well done! What a find. We must start using it now – *straightaway!*'

He called his men from the Manufactory to move the *Salvium* and spray guns, half to Caladrin Bridge and half to the jetty below Boar Hall.

'I'll stay with the men, if I may,' said the hermit. 'I need to take the cart back as soon as I can.' Everyone wished him well.

Mr Cringe took Sash and the Ravens to his office.

'Good morning,' said Peregrine as they sat down. It was time to catch up.

'Bring us your news,' said Mr Cringe. 'How has your plan been working?'

Logical Joe was eager to set the scene: 'First, we all think Lord Castus is about to return. Second, to weaken his support, Lord Tresquin has been exterminating the

Archers with a poison that comes from yellow frogs imported by Mr Haddock.'

'Benjamin Haddock?' said Mr Cringe. 'Responsible for supplying the poison? I can't believe it! He's as soft as porridge – and he's a solid Archer.'

'We think he sends the frogs away but doesn't know what they are used for,' explained Beth.

'Parcelled off to be used by a pernicious pig called "McFudgett",' said Sash sharply.

'Angus McFudgett? But he's on our side... You went there to get his help.'

Joe shook his head slowly: 'No, he is not on our side, Sir.'

'He tried to kill us!' said Sash.

Mr Cringe's eyebrows flew up and his mouth opened. 'What did he do?'

'You tell,' said Joe to his sister.

Beth described their sabotaged flight and how it had ended with their arrival at the hermit's dwelling.

Mr Cringe struggled to make sense of it all but was quick in his praise. 'Extraordinary! Remarkably brave, you two.'

'Sash did well, too, Sir,' said Joe.

Joe continued the story. He described what he had found, and what they had brought up from the bottom of the lift shaft. Beth added how they had helped Granelda, and how Mr Chelkwyn had developed sore eyes.

Mr Cringe listened well, but his mind was focused on using the antidote at once. 'How can we find out who else has been poisoned besides the Archers on our map?'

'I found this in the doctor's preparation room, Sir.'

Joe spread out the list of *Stonemasons' Targets* for everyone to see.

'There are more Archers here than we ever saw at meetings,' said Mr Cringe. 'Good people, friends… All poisoned! What sort of evil is this? How can we possibly help Lord Castus when he returns? Tresquin has troops that will far outnumber what we can raise.'

'But did you notice, Sir, that the doctor has poisoned Lord Tresquin as well?' said Joe.

'Lord Tresquin? Poisoned? By whom?' said Mr Cringe. 'Why would—'

Mr Pinwell burst into the room, looking pale. 'What's the rush? House on fire or something? I'm in a huge bake of mulberry cakes for the Citadel. Summon me when it's most inconvenient, why not?'

'Alhicbert, I'm sorry, but the heat's on for us to—'

'Yes, it *is* on! It's on my cakes – burnt to a crisp by now!'

Beth spotted the problem. 'I'm sorry, Sir,' she said, 'but I wonder if you have eaten anything yellow lately – or maybe you were given a yellow cream to rub on your skin?'

'What sort of question is that? Do I look jaundiced? Then again, who'd expect a sensible conversation with a stupid girl who can't even look after herself on a mission?' He glared at her.

'Alhicbert,' said Mr Cringe calmly. 'Beth thinks you

might have been poisoned. She's seen the early signs in Granelda, and we know the poison is yellow. Your position as past Secretary of the Archers has made you a prime target on McFudgett's hit list.'

'Granelda! My cousin, poisoned! How? And McFudgett? He's on *our* side! You're all going mad!'

'Would you partake of a drink, Sir?' broke in Sash.

'No! Yes! …I need something to dull the pain of being with such idiots.' He sank into a chair and closed his eyes.

The others looked at each other and nodded. The same plan had sprung into the minds of all.

'I'll be prompt, Sir,' said Sash. 'My father will help me prepare it in no time.'

Together they headed for the recent delivery of *Salvium*.

Mr Pinwell groaned, 'Oh, these knees… they are getting worse. I am aching all over.' He rubbed his legs. 'Tell me about Granelda.'

Joe and Beth explained about the yellow spray and how Granelda became irritable and stiff shortly before turning completely solid. Mr Pinwell kept accusing them of making it all up and demanded to see her, but he did not move. They reported their finding of the antidote and how they had given her some a few hours before.

'When Sash and his father bring you a drink, please do take it, Sir,' said Beth. 'It tastes fishy, but if it works, we will know that we can use it rescue all the Archers who have been poisoned.'

Mr Pinwell gave in. 'When in fairyland, do as the elves tell you,' he mumbled, looking more uncomfortable and weary by the minute.

Mr Cringe and Sash returned with a goblet of *Salvium* to which they had added some honey. Mr Pinwell spluttered, coughed and complained loudly, but he drank most of the purple liquid without spitting any out. A fishy burp followed, which he said was fitting for the occasion.

Within a few minutes he began to look brighter. He sat up to complain: 'Don't stare. I'm not a shop window.' He screwed up his face. 'My cakes! They'll be black, never mind me being yellow. Good*bye*!' With that, he managed his exit purposefully even with his creaking joints. Everyone cheered, not because he had left but because the antidote had already started to work.

The clock chimed – and clattered.

'Are we predicting a parcel, Pater?' asked Sash.

'No, but look inside anyway, please.'

'Nothing presents itself… oh yes, it does,' said Sash. He brought out a model sailing boat with a piece of paper wedged between its rigging.

'That looks like the ship I saw on Granelda's mantelpiece,' said Joe. 'Who is it for?'

'"To… the… Rav… ens… and… Mr… Cringe",' read Sash in an important voice. He handed the model to Joe and the letter to Beth.

Everyone stayed quiet as Beth tried to interpret the squiggly letters on its flimsy paper. As she did so, her face broke into sunlight. 'It's from Granelda! She has written to say she is getting better and can begin to move. Her legs "feel like a tinker toes" and her eyes are still misty. She thinks we will know what the ship means and has put in capitals just the word "TOMORROW". Then she's written a very large, "Love from Granelda".

Smiles and clapping erupted. The strong *Salvium* had worked. Granelda was being restored.

'What's a "tinker toes"?' asked Joe.

'A tinker toe is a man with a wooden leg. I suppose Granelda's legs are still feeling stiff,' said Mr Cringe.

'What is she telling us about the ship and "tomorrow"?' asked Beth.

'It fits with the return of Lord Castus,' said Joe.

'...pushing into the harbour,' said Sash with a flourish. 'Palatial! This is a model of a specially rigged ship for important events – usually for Persons of the Royal Family.'

'Is it armed?' asked Joe.

'It carries no guns, though the sailors have small firearms,' said Mr Cringe. 'It's a ceremonial vessel, but fully sea-worthy.'

'Surely it has protection?' said Joe.

'Yes. On the open seas it would have been flanked by fully armed galleons,' answered Mr Cringe.

'That's why Lord Tresquin sent all his troops to the Fortress, like the oarsman said.'

A knock on the door heralded the arrival of Mr Woollie. He was a tall man whose long silver hair was arranged vertically, as though reaching for the stars that he studied with his telescopes. With a waving gesture and a slight bow, he presented an invitation: 'I have set up my largest telescope for everyone to view the first of the triple conjunctions of Mars and Jupiter. It will be a magnificent sight.' Stars seemed to float out of his eyes at the thought. 'Five o'clock in the morning is the best time to see it. Refreshments will be available afterwards.'

'Thank you, Cyril,' said Mr Cringe. 'Not much notice, I'm afraid, when we have a lot to do ourselves.'

'My sincere apologies,' said Cyril dramatically. 'I would have mentioned it earlier, but I wrote a reminder on a handkerchief that blew into the furnace. Sorry. Lovely blue flames, though. Must have been the ink. Come if you can.' He disappeared through the doorway, bending his knees to avoid disturbing his astronomical hairstyle.

'That's the final confirmation!' said Joe, bubbling with excitement. 'That's what Castus said would be the sign – the conjunction of Mars and Jupiter!'

'Predication promised, playing out precisely. Plans now particularly pressing,' declared Sash. A supply of spotted Magnolia juice contained sufficient redcurrant fizz to energise them through a serious session of planning. What, exactly, should they do now?

CHAPTER 17

DROWNED

Very early next morning, a wiff barked three times outside Mr Pinwell's Bakery. He left his bread to rise, walked easily to the door and found a folded note:

Come to the Bridge at once.
Have sent wiffs to eighteen Archers who may still
be alive.
Six of them will join us, the others will meet at the
Manufactory.
I will bring the antidote.
Jarek Cringe

Mr Pinwell, transformed by the *Salvium*, moved quicker than ever before. Shouting to his wife to finish the day's baking, he left his shop faster than an angry bull. Mr Cringe joined him at the Inner Gate of Caladrin Bridge, bringing with him a handcart full of purple jars and loaded spray guns.

'We'll put these in the gatehouse,' said Mr Cringe. 'It's empty.'

'No guards?' asked Mr Pinwell.

'Orders of Lord Tresquin. All his soldiers have been sent to the Spykeeper's Fortress to head off any ship that could be carrying Lord Castus.'

'The devil! What's to do here?'

'Recover our stone-locked Archers. Get our people back to life for his arrival.'

'He'll have to get past the Fortress first. Needs to be in a ship like an East Indiaman. Fifty-six guns at least,' warned Mr Pinwell.

'Let's do what we can. We can't take on an army.'

Mr Cringe greeted the Archers that he had called to the bridge. There were only four, but each immediately took up a filled spray gun and ran to a marbled statue close by.

'What are the Archers at your Manufactory doing – if they're alive?'

'Going with Joe, Beth and Sash to Boar Hall. They're taking another batch of *Salvium* with spray guns. We've set wherries to take them down river. McFudgett's Stonemasons have put dozens of our poisoned friends on show along the Drive. They need reviving too – and quickly!'

'Too dangerous. They'll be seen from the house.'

'No, they won't. At this time of day, only the servants are awake and they'll be working in the kitchens. Sash will be a look-out from the side of the hall. He'll be armed with a bow and arrow. Beth will be nearby. She can trigger one of Joe's inventions to set fire to a pile of hay in the back courtyard. Joe's helping on the drive. If he needs to, he can climb up the ivy on the tower and ring the bell. He can throw stones at the greenhouse from there as well. That'll keep the household from looking down the drive!'

'And then?'

'Every Archer who has been restored will line the banks of the river to welcome our champion – or use their weapons to defend him.'

'Jarek, if this works, I'll believe in miracles. I'll do what I am told and stop thinking.'

Within an hour, much of the plan was underway. Mr Pinwell was in charge of the bridge. Mr Cringe, in the gatehouse, was distributing the *Salvium* to their helpers. The Ravens, Sash and seven Archers had taken jars of purple liquid with spray guns to Boar Hall. Many of the statues on the drive had already received their first shower of antidote. So far no one from the household had noticed.

Suddenly Sash spotted a man on horseback riding towards the back of Boar Hall. Beth had seen him too.

'That's Atticus Grobe!' said Beth, trying to whisper when she felt like screaming. Sash signalled to Joe, who sped at once to the bell-tower. Beth moved silently to her firing position and lined up Joe's laser with the dry hay bales.

The household stirred. A window opened.

Atticus rode his horse round to the back courtyard where came he came into full view. Breathing heavily, Sash loaded his bow. *Should I?* whispered an inner voice.

It is permissible! replied another voice in his head. *You are perfectly poised to punish this putrid person.* He pulled back the bow and, with shaky hands, took aim.

'Sash!' Beth whispered loudly as she ran towards him. 'Aim for the milk churn, not Atticus! He'll be really hard to hit on the move. The churn will make a noise and frighten the horse. That'll upset things enough!'

'*Beth!* Profoundly pleased you're here! I'm potty about you.'

'Yes, Sash, but don't let the arrows go to your head. I mean, Master Cringe, we are on a mission…'

'I'm pathetic at archery. Can you do it?'

A surprised Beth took the bow. Her arrow just missed Atticus and struck the old milk churn as planned. The echoing clang of its falling over made the animal rear up high and scream. Atticus fell. He hit the cobbled surface with a thud; after that, he didn't move. The horse ran into the courtyard where the smoke of burning hay spiralled round its nose and eyes. It whined loud and long.

Sash and Beth ran as fast as they could to the tunnel between Boar Hall and the river. On their way, a clanging bell rang out, then the sound of crashing glass. Joe had made it to the top of the tower. Nobody had chased after them, but in a short while footsteps clattered on the tunnel's stone floor.

'There you are!' A shout echoed through the tunnel. To their relief, it was Joe. 'I thought you might have forgotten we'd agreed to meet here after we'd set things up at Boar Hall,' he said.

'Us – never!' said Beth with a quick, knowing look at Sash. 'Here's your fire-raising torch.'

'Let's get back to the bridge,' urged Joe.

As they set off, their ears were hit by the sound of distant gunfire.

'That must be Tresquin's troops firing at the ship bringing Lord Castus,' said Joe, clenching his fists and hitting them together with rage. Suddenly, he wondered why on earth Castus had announced the time of his return. Surely he could have come back secretly and gained the advantage of surprise?

'Right,' he said. 'We may still lose, but we can't change the plan mid-action. We'll walk up the towpath to Caladrin to help there.'

When the bridge came into view, they faced a scene that was unbelievable: the Archers were returning to life! Joe shared his Omniscope with Beth and Sash to get a closer look. The white shine of the marbled Archers' faces and hands was fading to a shade of pink. Their eyes were growing clear, showing their usual colour, but they stayed wide open with fear for much longer. The statues' hair returned to normal and began moving in the wind.

Then came a more sudden change, as though their hearts had restarted. They took a sigh – only a small one. As the *Salvium* soaked into their agonised faces, their expressions moved through bewildered to cautious to jubilant. They blinked and looked around as far as they could while their necks remained locked.

At first, only a few Archers had been restored fully, but even those who could only move stiffly, or whose clothes were still hard, were already helping to spray others with antidote. Some were moving more freely, though apart from their heads, they still looked like statues. A few appeared normal but were weighed down by stone feet. Most of the children had recovered completely and were running to deliver refilled spray guns to the frontline team.

In the background, the crashing, war-like sounds of the Fortress battle could still be heard, though fewer cannons were firing than before. Then a strange roaring sound filled the air – the noise of a growing crowd moving downriver. Everyone was staring at the small, bright-coloured boat moving towards them with two people on board. One was rowing, though better dressed than any oarsman they knew; he also wore an unusually high hat. The other was sitting half-hidden under a blue canopy, a noble figure in a sequined coat of green, a tricorn hat and a fine plaited wig. He turned his head from side to side and occasionally raised his hand to give a royal wave.

'It's Castus! He's got through in spite of the fighting!' said Beth. The three let out a rousing '*Yes!*' At the same time, roaring and cheers from the crowd exploded. A chant began: 'Cas-tus! Back with us! Cas-tus! Back with us!' The noise grew as the boat approached – but where would it land?

A blink of bright light distracted Joe's attention. 'Look over there,' he said, 'on a mound behind the towpath where the river bends. It's the hermit!'

'Still in his cloak and hood,' said Beth.

'For protection!' said Sash. 'In case of pursuit, or poison or other peril. Probably.'

'I wonder why he's lit a fire?' said Joe, looking across with his Omniscope. 'There's an enormous bow lying on the ground, too.'

Sash's head was taking wider view of the scene. 'Peculiar sky,' he said. 'Puzzling. A thin grey cloud is approaching – a premonition of precipitation, perhaps?'

Joe swung his Omniscope to look round and up: 'No! *No!* It can't be true! The *scum!*'

'What?' asked Beth urgently. The sense of dread and anger in Joe's voice struck her with force.

'McFudgett! He's flying a balloon towards the river. He's painted grey and so is the balloon. It's the camouflage!'

'He's going to attack the boat, isn't he?' cried Beth.

Joe struggled to think clearly: *Position, resources, wind speed… Focus on…* 'Sash – can you swim?'

'Passably.'

'Across the river to the hermit, then. Tell him what's happening and that I'll shoot down the balloon while I can still see it.'

'How?' asked Sash.

'I don't care, anyhow you like: doggie paddle, breast stroke, upside down—'

'No, I really mean how—'

'...to get going? Like this.' Joe pushed him into the river. 'Best of luck. Try to breathe now and again.'

He watched for a moment to check that Sash could swim, then grabbed his PEST and commanded, '*IR Laser:100:3.*' All was completely fired up. As the camouflage dried, the balloon was disappearing rapidly; but it would be an easy target. He stood firm and took careful aim. '*Goodbye for all time, Doctor!*' he shouted, and with a pounding heart, pressed 'FIRE'.

Silence.

Nothing changed.

The balloon continued its slow approach towards the boat, unseen.

'*No! Why didn't it work?*' Joe screamed. He tried again. No effect. He looked intensely at his PEST. A flashing light at its base told him it hadn't been charged for four days: too little battery power left for the laser to work. He stared at the sky where the invisible balloon must have reached, He was horrified, helpless and felt utterly defeated. *Fool. I had the only chance of saving Castus and all these people, and I've failed.* The fireworks in his mind slowly fizzled out, replaced by a gloomy hollow.

Beth moved to his side. Nursing her own burning disappointment, she put her arm round his shoulder: 'We did our best, Joe. We solved the "curse", which is why we came. Look at all the recovered Archers…'

Across the river, Sash had been struggling. Before he reached the far edge his strength faded and he started to drown. 'Hold on! I'll pull you out!' the hermit yelled. Sash grabbed a rope that had just hit his head. He clung on, scrabbled up the bank and dripped onto the grass.

'Do you always arrive this way?' asked the familiar voice.

Sash was too waterlogged to speak but made a grunting noise by way of thanks. The hermit had already left him to run full speed back to the fire.

While the invisible balloon and its owner were still closing in on the boat, the growing excitement of the crowd echoed off Caladrin's walls. Most of the restored Archers had walked down the towpath to welcome their hero. The Archers from Boar Hall were streaming along the opposite bank to join the grand reception. A mixture of wonder, relief and hope was shown on every face. The royal barge bringing their rightful Duke to Caladrin – home after fifteen years.

With such a focus on Lord Castus, no one noticed the hermit standing tall with a bird on his shoulder and a bow in his hand. No one could have imagined what would happen next. Suddenly, the bird made an ear-piercing sound, like loud trumpets playing a ceremonial fanfare. It filled the air. People looked for a moment at the hermit before staring back at the royal barge. A huge cheer went up from the crowd. This must be the moment when Castus would reveal himself. The oarsman stood up. Yes! Something in the boat was about to happen. The man pulled hard on a rope. The canopy collapsed on top of his passenger. The stunned crowd quietened for moment then roared in disbelief and anger. Those who could began running down the towpath to rescue Castus from injury. Sash shook himself and joined them. The crowd descended into a riot when they saw the oarsman jump into the water and swim away as fast as he could. Several onlookers threw themselves into the river in pursuit.

No one in the crowd noticed that the hermit had lit a firebrand at the tip of a long arrow. Climbing onto the mound, he pulled back the string of his bow and sent its charge towards the invisible balloon. The brilliant white of the hydrogen explosion and its reverberating noise was followed by a deathly silence. The remains of the balloon and the basket caught fire and, with its unconscious occupant, fell heavily onto the boat. Everything sank within seconds. The stunned crowd watched a yellow liquid seeping across the river where the boat and Castus had disappeared.

CHAPTER 18

THE CROWNING ARROW

No one who witnessed the sinking boat could take in what they had seen. Castus had been drowned – the most noble, brave and generous man the land had known. The future they had desperately hoped for had disappeared in front of them.

Someone in the crowd shouted out, 'The hermit! He had a firebrand arrow!'

In a furious rage, the crowd turned round. They wanted revenge – a just death for a vile killing. Many already had weapons, and those who had none picked up brambles, sticks and stones. They rushed towards the cloaked figure with shouts of, 'To the death! Murderer! Traitor!' But as they came near, their leaders nearest to him were waving their arms wildly, standing in their way. They were shouting, '*Stop!* Put down your weapons! *Don't shoot!*'

Confusion everywhere. At the front, the crowd started shouting, 'Castus!' and, 'Long live our Lord!' At the back, anger was still propelling the crowd forward, crushing the people ahead of them. Gradually, everyone saw that the cloaked man had vanished. His robe and hood lay on the ground. The man in his place was wearing a majestic, olive-green coat with a sparkling silver thread. Castus stood tall with a calm authority and a wicked smile.

Now the crowd rejoined with deafening cheers, chants, flag-waving and even dancing. A small group of his followers built a stone platform for Castus to stand on. As he climbed up, the crowd broke into louder clapping and shouts of joy. It took a long time before they became quiet enough for him to speak.

'Thank you. Thank you everyone for your support. I am truly overwhelmed. Many people have helped me to return. Caladrin is my home and I am so very glad to be back!' His voice was no longer quiet but strong and assured.

More cheers.

'But… but I want first to say a special thank you to Mr Woollie – Mr Woollie, who made my mechanical stand-in with its clockwork-driven head and arm. He was also the oarsman that jumped ship, at the right time and at great risk.'

Mr Woollie appeared and was cheered. His hat had disappeared and his long silvery hair, flattened by the water, drooped all over his face.

'How has this all happened?' continued Castus. 'Deep plots were set against me long before the contest that gave the Dukedom to my twin, Tresquin. He had always been desperate to rule over you, and I know how much you have suffered.'

The crowd roared noise in assent.

'But there has been an even greater evil mind at work – a selfish, scheming mind hidden well by a great show of kindness and help to everyone. A charming man on the outside, but at heart, a venomous snake. He was the "bad blood" of our family – my cousin, Lentin. You might well have known him as Dr McFudgett.'

Lord Castus paused to look round at a few nodding heads in the silent crowd. 'He appeared most friendly towards my supporters… while, at the same time, he plotted with my twin to poison them before I returned.'

A roar of anger exploded and was slow to settle.

'But… but… as you see, their plans to prevent me returning have been foiled by a small number of brave and faithful people here: the Archers.'

A long cheer went up.

'More than that, we have been helped by two amazing children from far away.'

Lord Castus pointed to the Ravens on the other side of the river. 'You will not know them, but I extend to Joe and Beth my sincere and deepest royal thanks. Citizens of Caladrin and Boarham, without them we would not have succeeded, and many of you would have been statues for ever!'

The crowd roared and clapped until their hands hurt.

Though Joe and Beth were delighted, they felt even more uncomfortable than when Mother made outlandish noises in public.

Lord Castus continued: 'Is there any danger now? I say, "No!" The so-called "Dr McFudgett" has just fallen into his own poison. He will trouble us no more.'

The crowd cheered again.

'And the Duke, my twin? Poisoned by McFudgett in order to grab power for himself.'

The excitement and noise of the crowd became deafening.

Eventually, Lord Castus could speak again: 'Be assured: the ships that attacked the Duke's army at the Spykeeper's Fortress were those of McFudgett, not mine. To take over the Citadel he needed to defeat them. But countrymen, I can report that the two armies have completely eliminated each other. I am told that the Fortress is in ruins and the soldiers have fled. Both gunships have sunk.'

Yet more cheers.

'So, I bid you, good people, to go home. Let the purple antidote continue do its work. We will build a new community. Thank you again to my special helpers, including my son. Thank you all. I promise you a very different future.'

The noise of endless cheers rang out once more as the Archers made their way back to the bridge. Some wondered who the son of Lord Castus was – the young man standing close to him during his speech? They looked rather alike. A few also noticed the bird on Castus's shoulder, though talking about it later, they could not agree on its colour. Yet, these were details. Their bubbling joy was centred on their new Duke, Lord Castus, the *rightful* Duke of Curdlingshire. At last, a leader they could admire and trust.

As the crowd hobbled, walked or skipped back to the town, Mr Cringe pushed against the crush to meet Lord Castus and Sash. Across the river, Joe and Beth watched them closely. Curiosity-Joe grabbed his Omniscope to look at Lord Castus in close-up. His face came easily into view. In spite of all that had happened, the new Duke looked strong and peaceful, almost shining. And…

'Lord Castus has different-coloured eyes… Like Sash… and the "doctor",' he said.

'Different-coloured eyes?' said Beth, as though she had just understood the whole of algebra. 'That's what I saw in Lord Tresquin's portrait in the Citadel.'

'Then,' said Joe grandly, 'these must all be cases of *congenital heterochromia iridis*. I read something about it four years ago.'

'When you were seven?'

'…and a half.'

'Which means?'

'I'm really bright.'

Beth pulled a face a few centimetres from Joe's nose and said something like 'grandscoffenbiglyhead'. (He had probably heard that before.) With a voice of deliberate patience, she tried again. 'OK. What's the disease, O Master of All Knowledge?'

'It's having different-coloured eyes. It's inherited by all the men in one family. So, Sash must be the son of Lord Castus, not Mr Cringe.'

The conversation went quiet while they thought about what that would mean to the three figures climbing into another boat to be rowed back to town. Pain? Joy? Both? A huge surprise – or, just maybe, part of a plan hatched fifteen years before?

'Hello! It's been a great day, hasn't it?' A cheerful, high-pitched voice behind them interrupted their thoughts. They both turned around.

'Merrin!' said Beth, grinning widely. 'You're alive! And you look fine!' Whether or not it was proper to do so in the eighteenth century, Beth gave her a hug. Joe's face broke into a smile of growing relief and warmth.

'What happened after we saw you last? How did you get here?' asked Beth.

'When Granelda couldn't look after me anymore, I went to live next door to Mr Pinwell. I was in pain all the time. When he could, he sent some of the antidote to the town square and I recovered very quickly. I was desperate to find you and say, "Thank you." Thank you so much! Thank you for rescuing us. You *are* brave, and you *are* brilliant. I'm so sorry for the poisoned words I said.'

'Poison inside us often hurts others around. But you're cured! It's OK. And it's great to see you like this,' said Beth.

'The antidote *worked!*' said Joe, grinning.

'Coming back to Quince Cottages for lunch, my loves?' Granelda had come up behind and wrapped them in her arms.

They spun round to look at her. 'Granelda! You're back to normal, too! Your eyes look clearer than ever,' said Beth. Joe simply grinned like a pumpkin at Halloween. A recovered Merrin, a normal Granelda and one of her lunches: what a combination!

'You've completed your mission,' said Granelda. 'Thank you, and well done! When your courage and skill become fully known, the whole city will want to honour you. We would not have found the solution without your logic and inventions, Joe. Beth, you were prepared to help by becoming a servant rather than anything more grand – and you took to Thyripolis so well.'

'Joe's always been a whizz at gadgets – his flying tortoise found your presents in the first place.'

'Did they help?'

'They were life-saving,' said Beth, 'and without Joe's *Guide* we would have failed straightaway.'

'Joe?' said Granelda.

Joe took a breath in. *Focus on the data...* 'Yes... I don't understand how they work, but Beth's right. Without them we would be decomposing now and Dr McEvil would have won.'

'Did you see Thyripolis again, Beth?'

'Oh, yes! I didn't always recognise him, but he was around a lot. And he was on Lord Castus's shoulder just now, wasn't he?'

Granelda smiled. 'Yes. I think he was making sure that the burning arrow would line up with an invisible target, as well as giving Mr Woollie his cue to jump ship. Did you see Thyripolis, Joe? …Maybe not?'

Joe looked down. 'No,' he said quietly.

'Do you want to?'

That was the hardest question. A few strange expressions flitted across his face as he struggled to voice an answer. In truth, it was definitely 'yes' and definitely 'no'. But then, the scientists he had read about often made giant steps forward when they tried to understand something that everyone else thought was impossible. His brain signalled to his voice box: 'Maybe.'

'Well, here's an experiment,' said Granelda. 'Look hard at Lord Castus as he returns to Caladrin and see if you can sense anything out of the corner of your eye, to the right. That's where Beth and I can see him.'

Joe tried – with a mixture of feeling interested, silly, annoyed and afraid.

'Keep looking only at Castus,' said Granelda. 'No hurry.'

'All I can see is a blurred blob, sort of white.'

'Is it moving?'

'Yes… just a little, though maybe that's just the wind.'

'I think you've found him, Joe. And that's enough to start with.' Beth and Granelda exchanged smiles. 'Let's go back for lunch.'

On their way back to Granelda's house, Joe was cheerful near to bouncing, chatting with Beth and Merrin about their mother's outing and how *not* boring it had been. They enjoyed a fine meal together and learnt more about Sash from Granelda. He had been born abroad soon after Lord Castus had left England. A year after that his mother died of a snake bite, so Lord Castus sent him back secretly to England – to be looked after by Mr Cringe's family until he returned. Mr Cringe was a great friend and the first archery teacher Castus had.

'Did Sash know about this?' asked Beth.

'No, just in case his real father wasn't able to get back...'

'Won't Mr Cringe and Sash miss each other?' asked Beth.

'Yes,' said Granelda, 'but they will still stay very close. Now, I've got a surprise for you.'

In truth, Beth and Joe were surprised out after the adventures of the past week, but for kindness they sounded enthusiastic. 'I want you to hide in the clock, just for a moment...'

'But we *definitely* won't fit in!' said Joe in alarm, remembering his previous squeezing experience.

'I think you will this time. We've changed things.'

With difficulty, Granelda levered them in and pushed the door shut. The noise of the chime that followed was deafening, so much so that they had to push the door open at once.

They fell onto the staircase carpet of Boar Hall.

It was all very familiar. The clock showed a quarter

past one, the fortress was in ruins, the carpet was worn – and the clothes-rack had returned. They were back in the twenty-first century.

Their own clothes were *so* much more comfortable. And the OAK? Yes, it had come back too, though the PEST needed charging, of course.

They looked at each other with silent relief, and sadness. Memories of their adventures would tumble round their minds forever. Lunch? They would be late, but Mother wouldn't notice. Strangely, although they had only just eaten with Granelda, they felt hungry.

Soon, after a meal during which Mother found several other crazy relatives to describe, the Raven family drove along the drive away from Boar Hall.

'I've always *loved* those tall redwoods, and, sweet things, those *beautiful* flowers. My uncle Vince sent me a bunch on my twelfth birthday.' Mother was in good form, though her driving, as usual, was not.

Only one statue was in sight.

'Who is that?' asked Beth.

'Ah, that's Lord Tresquin. He's never looked very happy. Probably couldn't get his own way some time long ago. Mind you, I've seen so many people who—'

'I'm missing Sash already,' whispered Joe, 'though I could never decide whether he was really clever or not. I wish we could see him again.'

'Me, too. Maybe we will, another time?'

'Really?'

At home, Copurrnicus, curled up in the sunshine, purred at seeing the family return. Joe was more than pleased to see the silver bird back on its stand, though he looked at it in a different way now.

'Try staring into its eyes,' said Beth quietly.

Joe was still for a while, and then he did.

Thyripolis winked.

Joe winked back.